AF436161
Kah Wilde

A BARBARIAN WHO MUST LIE

When a prideful queen comes to his prison cell with an unbelievable proposal of marriage, Warrick of the Dead Lands is quick to accept … but not merely to secure his freedom. Because he recognizes the powerful jewels the queen wears — jewels pilfered from the temple of a goddess, who unleashed her wrath upon a kingdom. His plan? Pretend to go along with Queen Elina until he can steal the jewels back, then use them to lift the goddess's curse.

Except the queen isn't who Warrick assumes she is at first glance, and his deception might cost him everything…

A QUEEN WHO MUST DIE

Betrayed by everyone she's ever loved, trusting no one, Elina has spent years searching for the warrior prophesied to overthrow the sorcerer who stole her throne … and Warrick is the one warrior she's found whose description matches the prophecy. She doesn't want to marry a barbarian, but she's running out of time — the sickness ravaging her body means she'll be dead long before she sees home. Only the enchanted jewels she wears give her the strength to continue on … and her new husband's touch offers the only pleasure she's ever known.

But after a life spent running from those who betrayed her, Elina doesn't know whether to trust Warrick with her kingdom…or her heart.

THE
MIDSUMMER
BRIDE
KATI WILDE

THE MIDSUMMER BRIDE

ISBN-13: 979-8218266264

Printed by arrangement with the author.
For copyright inquiries, please contact:
Mick's Awesome Book Stuff
Melissa Khan, Owner
mick@micksawesomebookstuff.com

Cover and interior design by Kati Wilde

kati@katiwilde.com
www.katiwilde.com

FALERON
TAGDON
VALLEY OF STARS
GLASS MOUNTAINS
GALOTH

THE
MIDSUMMER BRIDE
Not to scale. Physical features and distances are exaggerated for clarity and fun.
THE DEAD LANDS
DARCOTH
TARROTH

ERE WE ARE AGAIN, WEAVING TALES OF BARBARIANS AND queens, picking up a thread spoken of long ago during a midwinter celebration. But the seasons have turned—so quickly, too quickly—and midsummer is finally here. In the days between, we have told stories of a kind queen, an ironskin queen, a champion queen, and a stonehearted queen.

Now comes a dying queen.

The time is anotherwhen, a date unknown but on the cusp of a curse's end. The place is anotherwhere, a world unnamed but too near our queen's destined grave. And this story begins, as many stories do, when all hope is nearly gone—

But, no. No time do we have for another rambling start! Quickly, let us begin. For we know that love is the most powerful of all true magics…but what use is love if she is dead? Hurry now, turn the page.

It might already be too late.

ELINA *the* CURSED

Torrath

"THE QUEEN'S FACE IS CRACKING," SAID CHARDRYN AFTER bustling into the royal tent and getting her first look at Elina in her finery. The old nurse clucked her tongue and continued, "Not even the promise of freedom will tempt an imprisoned barbarian to follow her if *that* is the visage he lays eyes upon."

Dara's narrow shoulders hunched slightly, but her steady strokes never faltered as she brushed gold paint onto Elina's chin.

The maid did not come to her own defense. So Elina did.

"The mask is too old, Chardryn." So thick and heavy as it dried that Elina dared not make more than the smallest movement of her lips to speak. "It was but a lump of paste in the bottom of the jar when Dara began. She salvaged what she could with the oils at hand."

The nurse nodded in resigned understanding. "Those at hand are not as refined as Aleron oils, I suppose."

Aleron. A pang of longing struck Elina's heart, as it did every time someone spoke the name of her kingdom. It had been far too many years since she'd left home. Since she'd *fled* from home, in truth—pursued by assassins sent by Soren, her sorcerer of an uncle.

"Well, no use fretting over what we can't change." Brusquely Chardryn set down her apothecary chest on the end of Elina's curtained bed. She opened the lid and fished out an assortment of herbs and powders. "No more of the queen's face can be procured until—"

"—we all return home," Dara finished with a wistful sigh. Abruptly her dark eyes widened and shot to Elina's. "Forgive me, Your Highness! I didn't mean to speak of—"

With her naked fingers, Elina gently touched the wrist that hovered near her cheek, the steady brushstrokes interrupted by the maid's dismay. "You've said nothing to forgive. The illness my uncle cursed me with will probably kill me before I return home. This we all know, and we need not pretend otherwise. But *you* will return, Dara. You *will* see your family again." Pulling back her hand, Elina smiled—though the stiffness of the paint only allowed a faint curve of her mouth. "Soon, if this barbarian is the warrior we seek."

If the barbarian was not, Elina might take him anyway. She had no more time to search for the warrior spoken of in the witch's prophecy. Better to return to Aleron with *any* warrior at her side than die far from home, having never attempted to remove her uncle from his ill-begotten throne or free her people from his tyrannical rule.

"Best not do more of that, Your Highness. Talking," Chardryn clarified when Elina gave her a questioning glance. "Smiling, too. Your face cracks all the more when you do."

"What of frowning, Nanny Char?" she teased the old nurse. "Or scowling? Yes, exactly in that way," Elina said when Chardryn demonstrated the same scowl that she'd often worn when Elina was a child, during those early mischievous years in the palace. Just as in those days, the nurse turned away to hide her smile, all the while muttering about disobedient and unruly charges.

"Once I'm outside, I'll not be able to help squinting under the bright sun," Elina added, only partially teasing now. Midsummer in the kingdom of Torrath brought with it a blinding heat.

"You'll not see a hint of the sun, child. We'll not let one ray touch the queen's face, lest it melt away. Here, now. Drink your tonic before she paints your lips."

Elina took the small cup, thinking that if not for the two attendants waving their enormous feathered fans to circulate air within the tent, the paint would have already melted away…and, weak as she was, Elina might have melted away with it. But the nurse's medicinal restorative would hold her together for a little while longer.

Though never long enough.

Made with water taken from a cold stream only that morning, the tonic was cool and sweet and utterly refreshing. Elina downed it in a few swallows that soothed her perpetually raw throat and instantly made her tender stomach protest. Blast it all. She battled the queasiness, breathing shallowly until the draught stopped trying to come back up.

"All right, then?" Chardryn took the cup, all the while examining Elina with a sharp eye.

Not yet completely trusting the tonic to remain inside if she opened her mouth, Elina nodded. But it was just as well. With her lips closed, they were ready to be painted. She looked at Dara—who in turn was looking at the three jewels that graced the fingers of Elina's right hand.

Again the maid gave a wistful sigh, though this time she said nothing.

Nothing needed to be said. Elina knew well what Dara was wishing. She'd often wished it herself. But the enchanted rings could not save Elina from her uncle's curse.

They *did* help her, however—just as Chardryn's tonic did. And they had already extended her life. Only two years past, she'd been on the cusp of dying, so weakened that her fingers could not hold a spoon and her belly could not hold a bit of food. Then the rings were delivered to her. Whatever magic was instilled in the jewels had bolstered her strength. Not enough to cure her, but enough to continue on…and later, when an assassin's arrow had bounced off Elina's chest instead of piercing her heart, she'd also discovered the enchantment protected her from any outside harm. The rings could not prevent *inner* harm, however, and the illness was already within her.

In the slow battle between the enchanted rings and the wasting disease, her uncle's curse was winning. All too soon, he would have his victory.

But not yet.

Finished with her lips, Dara stepped aside so that Elina could examine the result in the tall looking glass. The Radiant Queen of Aleron stared back at her, more resplendent and imposing in her traditional garb than Elina herself would ever be. Her long sickness had pared deep hollows and sharp angles into her features, yet when covered with the gold paint, those hollows and angles seemed sculpted instead of gaunt, regal instead of sallow. Her brown hair had been piled atop her head in an intricate arrangement of curls and braids, then liberally dusted with sparkling gold powder that concealed how brittle and limp her tresses were. The height of her hair was exceeded by a tall, stiff collar that framed her head in a nimbus of thin hammered gold, as if Elina carried the sun behind her instead of a curse within. From the collar draped a brocade robe, the thickness of the fabric disguising the frailty of Elina's frame; beneath the robe, an underdress of glistening gold silk gave to her movements an illusion of fluidity that her illness had stolen.

And Elina dreaded every movement to come, necessary though they'd be. She was already exhausted, her neck and shoulders aching from bearing the weight of the queen's traditional raiments.

She turned her head slightly, studying the queen's face in the mirror. The mask *had* cracked. Though not badly. Not yet. The gold wasn't fully smooth around her mouth and eyes, as if each smile and word left small wrinkles in the paint. Nothing could be done about that. Except to keep her expression as blank as possible and speak only a few words.

Fortunately she had someone to speak for her. "Please inform Serjeant Iarthil that I am ready."

Only a few minutes passed before Aleron's royal man-at-arms entered the tent. His stride hitched when he saw her in the queen's regalia. His throat worked and Elina espied a tearful gleam in his eyes before he blinked it away—yet not before his emotional response filled her heart.

Ten years past, Serjeant Iarthil had awoken a fifteen-year-old Elina in the middle of the night, a similar glistening in his eyes that the darkness hadn't been able to hide. But those tears had been from grief, not pride. He'd led her to the queen's bedchamber, where her mother was gasping her last breaths—poisoned by her own brother, Soren. With her final words, the queen urged Elina to flee from the palace, while Serjeant Iarthil swore an oath to the dying woman that he would guard her daughter with his very life.

It was he who'd gathered a retinue of dedicated soldiers and faithful companions to protect and accompany Elina—the true heir to Aleron's throne—until she could overthrow Soren's rule. It was he who'd led them from kingdom to kingdom, negotiating for asylum and forging alliances, until Elina was old enough to lead the negotiations herself.

In time, with a look here, a memory there—Elina came to understand that Serjeant Iarthil had not only served her mother but had loved her deeply, fiercely. Nothing had come of it, of course. Though he was the queen's highest ranking guard, duty had compelled her mother to marry the prince of a neighboring kingdom. Whatever their feelings, the honor of each had kept their passions bent toward serving Aleron.

But it meant that when he looked at her now, Elina knew not whether he was seeing her mother, who'd often worn this ceremonial garb, or if he saw Elina herself. Yet it hardly mattered. Either way, everything Serjeant Iarthil had fought for this past decade stood before him in resplendent robes. She lacked only one thing.

Two of the knights charged with guarding the royal strongbox had followed him into the tent, carrying between them a small chest emblazoned with Aleron's seal. Elina gave to Serjeant Iarthil the key she kept chained around her waist. He produced the second key. With a flourish, the double locks were opened and the lid lifted.

Her crown lay upon a bed of silk. No mere circlet, the Crown of Aleron was an ornate headpiece studded with precious jewels and made of pure gold.

And so very heavy.

Sudden weariness threatened to sag her shoulders. Instead Elina straightened her spine. She reached for the crown—and was stopped by Serjeant Iarthil's upraised hand.

"If I may, Your Highness?" he asked quietly. "Allow me to use my strength so that you may preserve yours."

Gratitude closed her throat, and she nodded.

Lifting the crown from the chest, he stepped in front of her. In the years since they'd fled Aleron, his hair had become fully gray and their travels had worn new creases into his face. In her more fanciful moments—and especially after realizing how he'd loved her mother—she'd imagined that Serjeant Iarthil was her true father, because he'd cared more for Elina than her mother's king consort ever had. The pale silver of Elina's eyes had been unmistakably inherited from the Prince of Tagdon, however, so those fanciful imaginings always fell apart.

"You are certain of this, Your Highness?" As he gently set the crown into place, his troubled gaze met hers. "Surely when the prophecy spoke of a barbarian who'd once worn chains, it meant someone other than an imprisoned thief awaiting execution."

Elina had thought it meant something else, too. She'd

thought her warrior would be someone like Kael the Conqueror, who'd once been in chains because he was stolen from the Dead Lands as a child and enslaved in the Blackworm mines. When he finally escaped, Kael had waged a bloody war against Geofry the Child-Eater, the cruel king under whose banner Kael had been taken. He'd killed the tyrant and freed the people of four kingdoms… and those people had begged him to take the throne.

In all the lands she'd traveled through, those four kingdoms had been the most prosperous and the people the most content. And Elina had hoped—hoped so fiercely—that a warrior such as Kael would return to Aleron at her side.

But she had no time left for hope.

"I am certain," Elina said. Completely, utterly certain that if she didn't soon return to her kingdom, she never would. The prophecy mattered little now. While she wouldn't ignore the witch's words—Elina needed every advantage when facing her uncle—she also couldn't afford to wait for a barbarian warrior to drop into her lap as her enchanted jewels had.

An imprisoned thief would have to do.

Despite her reply, Serjeant Iarthil pressed, "It is not too late to change course, but it will be once the proposal is issued. You will be bound by your vow."

"The serjeant only humors your quest to retake your throne, my queen. By his own vow, never will he lead you back to Aleron."

Unbidden, Lady Faraine's warning echoed through Elina's mind. Determinedly she shoved it away. Her mother's former lady-in-waiting had proved herself a treacherous companion, betraying Elina to secure her own comfort. The lady's words could not be trusted—and Serjeant Iarthil speaking his doubts and urging Elina towards caution was not an attempt to prevent her from returning home. *Of course* he shared his doubts about her marrying an unknown thief. He was protecting her. Keeping her safe. Just as she'd heard him vow to their dying queen.

So Elina would not heed that traitorous woman's warning. If Serjeant Iarthil was not loyal, if Nanny Char was not, Elina would have no one in the world left to rely on. And surely she could not be betrayed by *everyone* she loved?

Better that the curse take her first.

"I am certain," she repeated.

Though worry still darkened his eyes, Serjeant Iarthil nodded. "It will be as you decree." Then he gave to Elina a faint smile that lightened the heaviness in her heart and the weight of the crown. "Onward, my queen?"

As he'd said every time they'd left a place or encountered a new challenge. Only the increasing stiffness of the queen's face reminded Elina not to smile back.

"Onward," said she.

It was just as well that Serjeant Iarthil would speak for her while she wore the queen's face, because Elina could not have made herself understood. Though she'd learned several languages on this long journey, she didn't have the gift for them that Serjeant Iarthil did. At the prison, the warden spoke a dialect of the southern tongue that she could barely follow, and he claimed that the barbarian spoke it not at all.

"It's the only reason the beast hasn't met the executioner's axe." Clearly disgusted by the delay, the warden seemed about to spit on the dingy floor of his chamber, then glanced at Elina—who stood as silently as a statuesque figure made of gold—and thought better of indulging in such vulgar manners. "Lord Gleris still hopes to learn what happened to his stolen cargo. But no one speaks the eastern tongue."

"I will ask him," Serjeant Iarthil said mildly.

"You know it?"

"I do."

"Well, then. Gleris can't cry too much about what happens to the beast if I've got an answer for him. And no doubt the thieving fiend resold the whole lot." The warden glanced at Elina again. "Though I don't know that I ought to release him, no matter what you're willing to pay. He slaughtered the guards escorting the lord's cargo."

Yet he was imprisoned only for the theft and not the slaughter? What manner of priorities did these Torrathians have?

Elina's eyes narrowed. Seeing that slight reaction, the serjeant asked, "What was the cargo?"

"Ah…" The warden's tongue darted out to wet his lips. "Laborers."

Trepidation skipped over Elina's heart. Not laborers. They would never be called cargo. So he meant slaves.

She could feel no sympathy for this Lord Gleris or any guards who held people captive. Let them all be slaughtered. Yet she was troubled, for the warden assumed the barbarian had resold them.

They'd come for a thief. But was he also a murderer and a fleshmonger?

A look from Serjeant Iarthil said he shared the same worries. Yet they would know nothing if they did not meet this barbarian. And they would not meet the barbarian without the warden's cooperation.

Elina gave the slightest nod.

"We still wish to pay for his release," Serjeant Iarthil said.

"But at what cost to all of us, to release such a man? To let him loose upon this kingdom?" The warden dithered, shaking his head. "Such a decision should not be made so hastily. I must think of the people of Torrath. Of their safety, you see."

"We'll be taking the barbarian out of Torrath."

"I must also answer to Lord Gle—"

Serjeant Iarthil tossed a purse onto the warden's desk. When words were insufficient, Elina's gold spoke loudly enough.

The warden scooped up the purse with a sly grin. "Well, then. Let us go see if the beast wishes to be free."

As only Serjeant Iarthil and Elina had entered his chamber, the warden hadn't seen the score of knights and attendants who'd accompanied them. He briefly started upon encountering the two armored men flanking his door. His eyes widened before he nodded appreciatively. "A dozen knights ought to be enough to hold the beast. So long as you don't give him a weapon."

Serjeant Iarthil's brows rose. "Does he have a weapon? Were his possessions brought here with him?"

"They were. Horse and saddle. A few rags, some coin. And a big, bloody axe." If the warden noted how mention of the axe made several of Elina's knights and attendants exchange looks, he gave no indication of it. "The horse was sold to pay for his meals, the coin was…misplaced."

"We will take the axe."

"You're welcome to it. You there!" he called to a passing guard. "Hie off to the blade chamber, bring the beast's axe to Sir Ginarthil here." The warden seemed oblivious to the serjeant's dour stare upon the mangling of his rank and name. "Oh, I say—that's a fine way to get yourself about, your worshipness."

The last he said to Elina, who'd settled into her sedan chair, which was smoothly lifted by the four porters at the fore and aft poles. Chardryn fussed over her, making certain the skirts of Elina's robe and underdress draped just so before arranging the chair's curtains to best frame the golden figure sitting inside.

Elina despised being carried about in this way. But

she had little choice. Simply walking from the entrance of the prison to the warden's chamber would have sapped her strength. Attempting to walk the full distance to the barbarian's cell whilst wearing her heavy crown and raiments would be near impossible.

The litter served another useful purpose, however, by declaring her status and her wealth. Elina hoped to tempt a thief. Showing the barbarian thief that she was absurdly rich could only help persuade him.

At a nod of her head, the porters started forward. From the attendants trailing behind, Elina heard whispered mentions of the axe and the prophecy—all spoken in tones of rising hope.

Elina didn't dare hope. She did not dare. Yet her heart pounded ever harder the farther into the prison they went, her blood surging at a dizzying pace, the witch's words spinning unspoken over her tongue with every breath.

You will know it is he, wandering queen, because from the moment he first lays eyes upon your face, his heart will forever after compel him to follow.

His heart. Forever after.

If the witch had spoken true, Elina would be loved.

And if this was the warrior she sought, Elina would be loved very soon. The moment he looked at her. She longed for such a love until she ached.

But she didn't dare hope.

The warden led them into a dank, narrow passageway. A rotten stench filled Elina's next breath. Gods, no. This was *not* how her warrior would first look upon her—puking onto her golden slippers. In years past, she would not have even blinked at such a smell. That was before the curse and the illness made her stomach turn inside out at the slightest provocation. She gagged and fought her rising gorge, then almost cried her relief when Chandryn pressed a perfumed kerchief into her hand.

Ahead, the warden and Serjeant Iarthil had stopped in front of a wall made of iron bars, while her chair had not yet been carried beyond the shadows in the passageway.

The prisoner inside the cell wouldn't be able to see her yet.

"Hold here," Elina choked out, then put the kerchief as near to her nose as she could without smearing the queen's face. May the gods forever bless Nanny Char, for the nurse had not doused the silk with an overpowering floral or musky fragrance, but with peppermint that cut straight through the stench.

Her breathing eased. Her eyes adjusted to the dim glow of the single lantern lighting the antechamber. Other cells they'd passed had narrow slits in the stone walls to let in air and light. But no slits opened the walls of the barbarian's cell, and she strained to see beyond the bars.

Her heart leapt into her throat as movement in the shadows accompanied the slithering of iron over stone. No true sight of him yet. Only the impression of something…big.

Serjeant Iarthil had a better view inside. Disquiet

marked his voice as he asked, "You keep him chained even behind bars?"

"We must." The warden stepped forward to nudge one of the bars—which rattled loosely in its anchor of stone—before moving swiftly back. "One pull, and he nearly ripped that one out. The chains don't let him near enough to grab hold of them. Or us."

"I see." The serjeant moved closer to the bars.

"Careful, Sir Ginarthil!" The warden urged before sharpening his voice. "Beast! Come and show your face! And don't you give any trouble, for a goddess is here to set you free. They paid a heap of gold for you."

Elina could almost feel Serjeant Iarthil's exasperation. The warden must have, too.

Defensively the man said, "I'm just calling him forward. He doesn't understand a word, but he understands tone just fine. Just like a dog does."

"Yet I do not see him come forward." Turning back to the bars, Serjeant Iarthil spoke in a language she'd heard a few times in port cities along the Illwind Sea. In his youth, the serjeant had sailed east of that sea—nearer to the Dead Lands, the home of the barbarian clans, though he'd never entered that barren realm.

"What did you say?" the warden demanded.

"Only that I wish to speak with him. That I have a proposal for him," the serjeant replied. Elina knew he answered for her sake, not the warden's. He would translate for her everything that was said.

Another rattle of chain—louder, quicker. Then suddenly he was there, looming out of the shadows. Elina sucked in a breath. The cell was too dim to see him clearly, yet her impression of size held true. The barbarian was *massive*. Not only taller than Serjeant Iarthil by a full head but heavier, too. Wider shoulders, broader chest. All thick muscle that was impossible not to see, for a rag knotted at his waist provided his only covering. The lantern's glow illuminated expansive swaths of skin smeared with dirt and the gods knew what else. Manacles gleamed dully at his wrists.

She could see nothing of his features or his eyes. Even if the dim lantern had allowed it, dark tangles of hair hung in his face.

Her skin prickled when the barbarian spoke. His voice was low and rumbling and *deep*, as if each foreign word came from the back of his throat instead of the tip of his tongue, as Serjeant Iarthil's did.

The serjeant answered him in the same language, then said, "He asks what proposal I have. I told him that we could secure his release in exchange for a service done."

A service. Elina wished to be more than a service. Or a duty.

But she did not dare hope.

"You offer release too hastily, sir," the warden said. "Make certain he knows the executioner awaits unless he confesses what he's done with Lord Gleris's cargo."

As the serjeant conveyed that, everything within Elina

tightened, stilled—waiting for the answer. If the barbarian *had* resold the slaves, she would leave him to rot in his cage. Prophecy be damned.

The barbarian's reply was short. "He asks what moon rose last eve."

"The moon? What has that to do with anything?"

Serjeant Iarthil shrugged lightly before answering. He offered no translation but Elina knew what it was. *Full.* Last eve's moon had been a full moon.

The lantern's glow caught a flash of white teeth as the barbarian grinned. Amusement filled the rumble of his reply.

Relief filled Serjeant Iarthil's. "He says that this dawn saw the cargo upon a ship, sailing back to their homes as free women and men."

Constricting doubts eased their tight hold upon Elina's heart. Happiness swelled within. For although she'd dared not hope, this barbarian *was* like Kael the Conqueror—and exactly the sort of warrior Elina needed at her side. He'd freed Lord Gleris's slaves. Surely he would help free her people, too.

Elina hardly recalled commanding the porters to carry her forward and to set down her chair. Under the weight of her crown and robes, rising from the litter took all of her strength and left her trembling with effort—yet she would not let him see her weakness. Not yet. Soon enough he would know. But in this moment, she only wanted him to see the resplendent, imposing queen. Stiffening her spine, raising her chin, she stepped into the lantern's glow.

He could see her face now. Though she could see almost nothing of his. Only the gleam of his dark eyes, narrowed upon her as he looked through his filthy tangle of hair.

Then the widening of those eyes…and the fierce joy within.

For the first time, she dared to hope. Stepping forward, she heard Serjeant Iarthil announcing her to the barbarian as the Radiant Queen of Aleron, who had a proposal for him.

Her proposal. Which according to Aleron custom, the queen had to make—it could not be spoken for her.

Elina prayed that she would not puke.

She moved the scented kerchief away from her nose and tried to speak the traditional words all in one breath. "Warrior of the Dead Lands"—truly she ought to have learned his name first—"I bestow upon you the honor of offering to you my hand in marriage, that you may be joined in glorious matrimony to the Radiant Queen and be named her splendid consort." Oh gods, the stench wafting from his cell was worse than any she had encountered yet. Her stomach began to heave. Desperately she steeled herself to finish. "Warrior of the Dead Lands, will you vow to lovingly submit your flesh, seed, and heart to serve and protect the golden queen and all the citizens of her kingdom? Will you accept the honor of my hand?"

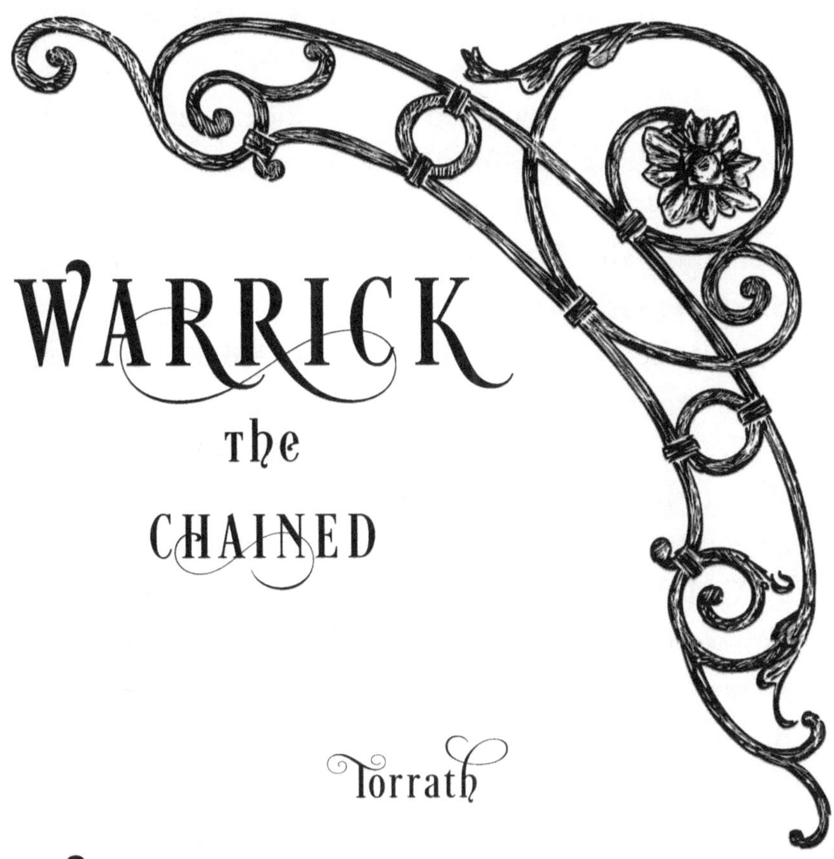

WARRICK

THE

CHAINED

Torrath

"WILL YOU ACCEPT THE HONOR OF MY HAND?"

Marry this prideful, haggard *monstrosity*? If Warrick's joy at seeing the Stars of Anhera on her fingers had not already bled into fury, he would have laughed in her golden horror of a face.

Best that he did not. Laughing *before* the queen's man could translate her proposal would reveal that Warrick understood her northern tongue as well as the eastern tongue—just as he perfectly understood the warden's southern tongue.

He hardly listened as the serjeant began relaying the proposal. Marry her? No. He would kill this gilded monstrosity for what she'd done to the people of Galoth when she'd stolen Anhera's jewels.

Though killing her would not be easy. Not while she wore those rings. And they could not be taken from her. She had to remove them willingly.

But the monstrosity might remove them for a man she meant to marry.

"Why marry a convicted thief?" he asked when the serjeant had finished the recitation. "Your queen cannot even tolerate the smell of me."

Only with effort did Warrick keep the sneer from his expression. She'd removed the gold silk from her face long enough to propose. Now she breathed the perfume again, her every inhalation a grotesque, wet gulping.

"He asks why you chose him," said Iarthil in the northern tongue—which the warden spoke not a word of. With grim amusement, Warrick watched confusion overtake the warden's fool face, yet the man did not interrupt. Instead he stared at the golden monstrosity with a deference bordering on awe.

A goddess, the warden had called her. Was that what she believed herself now, wearing a true goddess's rings? If so, she was a goddess of sickness and death and greed. Exactly the sort the warden would worship.

Her response was muffled by the silk kerchief held between her bejeweled fingers. "Tell him of the witch's prophecy. Tell him we seek a barbarian in chains so that his axe might fell my uncle." Her voice quavered slightly.

"But do not say how we will know whether he is the right warrior."

Prophecy? Not one spoken by a true witch of the Dead Lands, that was certain. No one from that realm would ever use magic for so frivolous a reason as fortune-telling.

"She requires a warrior from the Dead Lands to remove the usurper on the Aleronian throne," Iarthil told him. "Her kingdom lies north of the Glass Mountains and is home to riches that most cannot even dream of. You would be well rewarded for your acceptance of her proposal."

Warrick's eyes narrowed. "If she owns such wealth, then she only need hire a warrior. Not marry one."

Iarthil hesitated before saying, "The queen has not long to live. In the eyes of Aleron, a widowed king consort who secures his queen's throne to fulfill a vow will be celebrated. Whereas a mercenary warrior who slays the usurper will be called an assassin."

Not long to live. That was certain.

Yet now Warrick looked at her more closely. She was of advanced years—of that there could be no doubt. Though she'd attempted to conceal her age with a gold mask, the paint had settled into every wrinkle and crease in her skin.

And her eyes. He couldn't make out their true color in the dim light, yet their watery paleness suggested her sight was clouded by cataracts and time, with a pinched tightness at the corners that said she rarely appreciated the sight of anything she looked upon.

Those were unmistakably the eyes of a bitter old woman.

Which likely explained why, ten years past, she'd stolen Anhera's jewels. Feeling her age, hoping for immortality, uncaring of anyone else. Mayhaps the goddess's stars had given her strength. But if she was nearing death after only a decade, they'd not given her enough.

To tack a scant few years onto the tail of a selfish life, she'd cursed an entire kingdom.

Yet apparently her greed had no limits, for even at the end of her life, she wanted to claim a throne. And use Warrick to do it.

Mayhaps she wished to use him for more than that. Disgust shriveled his balls when he witnessed the lewd crawl of her rheumy gaze from his chest to his thighs.

But that interest could be used against her.

Suddenly Warrick knew exactly how he might relieve her of the jewels. "Is your queen still a virgin?"

Offense stiffened the serjeant's expression. His outraged glare was his only answer.

"If she is, know that she will not be after we wed. I will not take a wife that I cannot fuck."

A muscle in the serjeant's jaw twitched. Again, he did not respond.

The monstrosity did. "What does he ask?"

Face rigid, Iarthil struggled for a moment, as if searching for the proper words. "He asks if you are untouched, my queen. He wishes for a true marriage."

Her gaze flew to Warrick's. He could not mistake the revolting eagerness that sparked in her eyes. "Assure him that I am a maiden and that he may share my bed."

"I will share her bed beginning this night," said Warrick when her response was relayed.

Without consulting his queen, Iarthil shook his head. "You will not be wed yet. Not for five days hence."

"Then I will not fuck her until we are married. But I *will* share her bed."

"You will *not.* The Radiant Queen is only to be touched within the bonds of marriage." Abruptly the serjeant's rigid control snapped and he spat, "Have you no respect, warrior? If you wish for a whore to use, reject my queen's proposal and I will see that the warden sends onc to you."

"Serjeant?" Though her voice rose nasally, as if she pressed the silk harder to her nose, with that single word she demanded to know what was being said.

Bright pink overspreading his face, the man closed his eyes and drew a deep breath before turning to her. "He wishes to sleep at your side, Your Highness. Beginning this night."

"He knows that I must be a maiden at my wedding?" The query was followed by another wet gulping.

"He does."

"Then he may."

Fiery satisfaction rolled through Warrick's veins. "I will wed her, then."

Chin high, she gave a single, regal nod after Serjeant Iarthil translated Warrick's acceptance. Then she turned and retched, spitting out a thin and stringy mess onto the stone floor.

"Her chair!" Iarthil barked, catching her crown as it toppled from her head.

The porters rushed forward with her litter, followed by a stout, gray-haired woman who fluttered like a ruffled hen around the heaving queen. The gilded monstrosity wiped her mouth and clambered shakily into her chair. Quickly the fluttering hen drew the curtains closed but could not shut out the sound of the queen's gagging and gasping for breath.

"Escort the queen outside and into the fresh air, Nurse Chardryn. I'll finish here." With the crown tucked against his side, Serjeant Iarthil waited until the gaggle of attendants had disappeared into the passageway before turning back to Warrick. "I suggest that you bathe before you come to her."

Warrick would more likely need to bathe after. His own stomach heaved at the thought of touching her. Her age was no impediment. But he had hoped to at least respect the woman he finally bedded.

Yet too much was at stake to let his revulsion show. He could not risk losing the jewels. And he need not fully fuck her. Only make her crave his cock so badly, she would make herself vulnerable.

"Did you find the axe?"

The warden spoke as one of the measly-faced guards appeared, lugging a sack over his shoulder. The straining burlap had been sliced open by the heavy object within, a curved razored edge gleaming in the lantern light.

His old friend. Warrick grinned.

The guard let the sack thunk to the stone floor. He flicked open the burlap, showing to the warden the head of a steel battle-axe.

Iarthil looked to Warrick. "This is yours?"

"It is."

"It has no handle."

Because one of Gleris's guards had known some small spells and had crumbled the handle to dust. It hadn't mattered. Warrick hadn't needed an axe to split the man's skull.

He also didn't need a handle to swing the axe. Not when something just as useful was at hand.

Wrapping the heavy links around his wrists, Warrick hauled back on the chains securing him to the stone wall. In an explosion of gray dust and stone chips, the iron loop anchored in the wall's mortar gave way. The warden cried out for him to desist, then scrambled back as Warrick approached the bars. The prison's abundant rat population had kept Warrick well fed—and had given him fleas—but now served another purpose. Ignoring the fool warden, he swept up a rat bone from the floor. With it, he opened the lock on his cell, then his manacles. He tossed them aside.

The chains he kept, coiling the iron links before looping them over his shoulder.

Through it all, Iarthil stood his ground, regarding him impassively. Likely wondering why Warrick had remained imprisoned when clearly he could have escaped.

Yet he didn't ask. Instead he tossed to Warrick a heavy purse. "Buy for yourself a horse, clothes, weapons—whatever you require for a long journey—but do not discard that axe. Bring it with you. When you've secured your supplies, there is a road that follows the river north out of the city."

"I know of it."

"We intend to make camp at the three waterfalls that lie a half day's ride north—and will expect you before the evening star rises. Make no attempt to approach us after dark, for I will not lower the camp's defenses and risk any threat to my queen's safety. If you're late, wait for dawn."

Was he hearing aright? Warrick was to be left alone to buy what he needed and then catch up to the queen's escort? By its weight, the purse held a small fortune. Much more than required for a good mount and clothes. What was to stop Warrick from taking this and riding his new horse in the opposite direction?

Only his word.

Which meant that this was a test.

Warrick had seen the serjeant's relief when he'd learned Gleris's slaves were freed. Iarthil likely considered himself a man of honor. But he could not truly be. Not if he bound his honor to someone such as his queen.

Warrick's honor was not bound to anyone. Instead it was bound only to what was right.

At this moment, that meant doing whatever necessary

to return the Stars of Anhera to the goddess's temple and break the curse that afflicted an entire kingdom.

"I will be there before night falls," he said.

"WARRICK!"

Bannin called out from a corner of the tavern where he and Warrick had arranged to meet on the morning after the full moon. Judging by the number of trenchers and mugs littering his table, the big red-haired warrior looked as if he'd been settled there for a while.

The tavern wasn't even half full, and the patrons who were there seemed seated as far as possible from Bannin. Now their wary eyes took in Warrick—a burlap sack and chain over his shoulder, on bare feet and scratching at his flea-infested hair, coming directly from the prison.

Like a spider, the innkeeper skittered forward to intercept him—likely thinking to toss a filthy cur out on his ass—then appeared to think better of that intention when the size of that filthy cur sank in.

The innkeeper wrung his thin, bony hands. "Ale, sir?"

"Two."

"Is another joining you?"

"Both for me." He flicked the man a gold piece that could buy a year's worth of ale for every patron within. "That also ought to cover whatever my Golathan friend has had."

"Yes, sir!" Clutching the coin, the innkeeper hurried away.

"I expected you hours ago." Bannin smirked as his gaze ran Warrick's length. He paused on the chain. "Trouble getting out?"

"None at all." Dropping onto the bench seat, Warrick snagged a hunk of bread then swiped it through the gravy congealed at the bottom of a trencher. "I became so fond of my cell, I took part of it with me."

"Confess, man. You—" Abruptly Bannin jerked back in his seat, breath gusting out. "Oick! A chain wasn't all you brought with you. The smell of you could fell a horse!"

Or a radiant queen. But only if she puked to death. "Could it fell Lord Gleris?"

"No need. I slit that slaver's throat as soon as they sailed—and it was just as we hoped. Gleris's men never even came looking for us at the docks. Never figured out there were two of us or that they ought to be looking at me, because they were so focused on getting answers from you." Leaning in, Bannin lowered his voice. Only half in jest, he asked, "You don't see Gleris, do you? He's not floating behind me, looking for vengeance?"

With his craw stuffed full of bread, Warrick couldn't speak. So he answered by leaning back and giving Bannin a good eyeful of his bare chest.

No glowing. So no ghosts.

"Merciful gods, don't lift your arms! With such a stench, you'll put me off meals for a week." Bannin rose, ale in hand. "Let's take this slop outside so I can breathe, yeah?"

Warrick froze mid-nod. The fingers Bannin had slipped

through the handle of his mug were gray—and stiff. His gaze flew to Bannin's.

"Don't," the man snapped, his voice a thick rasp. "Save your sympathy for the others. Give none to me, who failed them all."

Bannin hadn't failed anyone. But the bread wedged in Warrick's throat and the dull ache in his chest kept him from replying. He followed Bannin outside, where the midday sun was a blinding glare after a month spent in the dark.

An awning provided shade over a square wooden table, though a nearby stable put into doubt any improvement in smell. The innkeeper set down Warrick's ale and skittered back inside.

"When?" Warrick asked.

"A few days after we took Gleris's caravan—it's my blasted sword arm, too. But I figure I've got half a year before the stone reaches my heart." His jaw worked. "It doesn't matter what happens to me. Helana wrote. Ouin's got the sickness."

Helana, his sister—and Ouin, his nephew. When the boy was a babe, Helana's husband had fallen to the stone sickness—but he hadn't left her bed. He was still there, a statue frozen at his final breath. Helana hadn't let Bannin move him.

In the past ten years, Galoth had become a kingdom of statues.

Bannin drew a trembling hand down his face. "It's up

to Ouin's knees. She says his feet are fully…and he can't—"

His words choked to a stop. The boy was but five years of age, born after the Stars of Anhera were stolen and the curse began. The sickness struck the people of that kingdom without care or mercy, slowly turning an entire body to stone. In early years, when the sickness became apparent in someone—at the tips of their fingers or their toes—many had attempted to stop its spread through a limb by cutting it off. But the sickness merely spread from the stump. There was no cure and no way to stop it.

Except by breaking the curse. "I found the stars."

Bannin scoffed and wiped his eyes, but rallied as if he thought Warrick was leading him into a joke and he was eager for a diversion. "Stuck in the walls of your cell? Did a friendly rat bring them to you?"

"An old haggard queen, draped in gold and a crown and paint."

Bannin blinked. "I heard tell of a gold goddess being carried through the streets this morn."

"Not a goddess—though she likely thinks herself one. She wears the rings."

His friend's grin was sudden and fierce. He shot to his feet. "Not for long."

Warrick clamped his hand onto Bannin's arm and shoved him back into his seat. "Go home. To Helana and Ouin."

"Not without—"

"I'll bring the jewels to you." When he saw Bannin

open his mouth to argue, Warrick headed him off. "She can't be killed when she's wearing them. She has to trust me. To give them to me. If you march in swinging your sword, she never will."

"She'll trust you? A hulking brute?"

"She wants to marry me."

Bannin stared at him. "Marry you."

Warrick nodded.

"You're saying to me that some ancient queen came to your cell, fluttered her lashes and said 'Oh please please marry me, you big stinking barbarian'?"

She'd puked rather than fluttered. But otherwise Bannin's rendition was fairly accurate. "Then she bribed the warden to secure my release."

"You're tugging my prick."

"It's no jest. I am to kill her uncle and win her a kingdom."

"Which?"

"Aleron. You know of it?"

"I do." Disgust twisted Bannin's mouth as if he'd gotten a whiff from under Warrick's arms again. "It lies north of Galoth. Over the Glass Mountains. Ruled by a murdering tyrant whose only care is gold."

"The niece seems little different."

Bannin grunted in response to that. Then his eyes narrowed as he said slowly, "As I recall, when the curse first began the rumor in Galoth was that the new king of Aleron had stolen the stars—or that he'd hired someone to steal them. But those who were sent to Aleron reported that the jewels were never seen in his possession. And they *would* be seen. The rings have to be worn or they offer no protection."

Rumor had not been far off. "They looked to the wrong member of that royal family."

"Seems so. She wants you to kill him? He's a dangerous bastard. Sorcerer, I've heard. And there's enough gold in that kingdom to pay for what his magic can't do, so you being impervious to spells won't be enough to save you."

"It matters not." Warrick wouldn't be traveling to Aleron. "I'll have the jewels within the fortnight."

"How?"

"She wants to wed in five days."

"On Midsummer Day?"

Warrick knew not what day it was—yet that likely explained why they intended to wait. Otherwise there was no reason not to marry this same night. "She claims to be a virgin. I can't break her maidenhead if she's wearing the rings."

"*That* is your plan?" Bannin snorted out a laugh. "You know nothing of women. Not all virgins have maidenheads that need breaking."

"She'll hardly know whether she does or not. I'll pretend I can't get my fingers in, let alone my cock." Warrick didn't want to get into her anyway.

Bannin laughed at him for a minute longer. "Good luck to you, my friend. You'll bring the jewels directly to Galoth?"

"I will." Dropping the queen's purse onto the table, Warrick fished out a few coins—more than enough for a horse and boots, and a journey to Galoth after he had the stars. "Buy passage on the river. Do what you like with the rest."

The river route would carry his friend home—to Helana and Ouin—much faster than traveling by road.

Bannin took the purse, eyes widening when he hefted its weight. "She gave you this?"

"Her man-at-arms did."

"Did he *want* you to run?"

Warrick hadn't considered that. He'd assumed it was a test of his honor. But Iarthil had also pushed him from the queen's bed at every turn. Mayhap the serjeant feared that another warrior would usurp his place at the queen's side.

But it mattered little, since the queen would soon be dead.

The sound of a ragged breath pulled Warrick from his ponderings of all the satisfying ways he might kill her. Bannin was staring off into the distance, eyes glistening, his throat working.

"All that time we spent searching for those jewels. Every rumor we chased leading to nothing except ghosts and the evil bastards we had to put down with our blades. All those years, and now it's your cock that'll break the curse." He shook his head, gave a mirthless laugh. "I ought to have known how it would be. While waiting for the ship and keeping those people hidden from Gleris, and with you stuck in that prison, then reading Helana's letter—I'd begun to regret…well, not regret freeing them. But that helping them had halted the search. And resenting that it was all taking so long. Then I'd hear you in my head, saying 'you'll never regret doing what's right' along with all the rest of your son-of-a-witch Dead Lands horseshit. So many nights I spent lying awake, my fingers turning to stone, wishing you would shut your mouth. Yet if we hadn't helped those people, if waiting for the ship hadn't delayed us and kept us in Torrath, we wouldn't have been here at the same time as this queen."

"Be certain I'll be saying that horseshit more often now."

The laugh that broke from Bannin ended on a breath like a sob. "The jewels *are* the stars?"

The desperate hope in his friend's eyes wrenched at Warrick's heart. "I'll bring them to you, brother. This I vow to you. By summer's end, I'll deliver the jewels to Galoth. Along with her golden head."

"I'll drink to that." Bannin lifted his mug. "To doing what's right?"

Warrick grunted his approval. "To doing what's right."

And to breaking curses with his cock.

ELINA the BREATHLESS

The Falls

"WE ARE NEARING THE CAMP, YOUR HIGHNESS," Serjeant Iarthil announced from his mounted position beside the carriage, rousing Elina from stupor to anticipation.

The camp was one they'd used before. The site was well-situated at the base of an escarpment, over which tumbled three streams that splashed into a wide pool before narrowing into a single river. A cooling mist continually drifted off the waterfalls. Colorful flowers blossomed upon every cliff ledge, their fragrances gently perfuming the breeze. If Elina's strength allowed, she hoped to sit upon the small boulders that ringed the pool, breathing in that lush air.

Her strength would likely not allow. With every rut and bump in the road, the tonic sloshed uneasily in her stomach. The sun beat down upon the roof of the carriage and, despite opening the curtains, the air within was stifling. In her brocade and paint, Elina could hardly breathe or move, as if she were being slowly smothered by the queen's raiments.

But more torturous would be the hours until nightfall. Wondering whether the barbarian warrior would follow her.

He would not need to. The purse she'd given to him held a fortune in gold. Even if he never laid eyes upon her again, he could live like a king for the remainder of his life.

Though he did not seem the sort to flee an obligation. The serjeant had told her how the barbarian had broken his chains and opened his cell. Which probably meant he'd been biding his time within the prison, waiting for the ship to sail and for the men and women he'd freed to be out of harm's way.

Elina lifted her head from her pillow. "Serjeant Iarthil."

Never distant, he drew his horse closer to the window of Elina's carriage—which was more properly a wheeled lounging bed with seats for her attendants. In early years, before the curse, she'd ridden her own horse beside his.

She missed those days.

"Your Highness calls?"

"Did you learn the warrior's name?"

"Warrick of the Ghost Clan."

Warrick.

Who wanted to bed her. The very thought made Elina feel meltingly hot—not the horrible smothering heat, but a warmth resembling honey, thick and sticky and sweet.

Though perhaps it was only the queen's face that had sparked his admiration—and now that face was also melting, but into a horror. Elina prayed he would not be put off by her own features, for she rarely wore the paint.

She also prayed he hadn't been put off by her puking.

"I wish to bathe as soon as we arrive."

"Of course, Your Highness," said Dara.

"And wear the lavender silk after."

The maid exchanged a glance with Chardryn. Never had Elina worn the lavender, for it was nothing but a wisp of a gown.

"And I would share my supper with Warrick. A picnic by the water." If he arrived in time for supper.

Chardryn frowned. "Your Highness—"

"On a blanket." Elina countered the objections she knew would come. "With cushions. It will take no more effort to sit there than lying in this carriage does. And the attendants' tent must be raised."

Usually Nanny Char and the maids kept quarters in Elina's expansive tent. Not any longer.

"What if he does not come?" Serjeant Iarthil asked.

Her heart constricted at the thought, and it hurt to pull in a breath. As if her very lungs were being crushed. "Then…onward. Do *you* think he will not come?"

The serjeant had spent more time with Warrick than

Elina had. He'd been able to speak directly to him. His impression of the barbarian would be deeper than hers.

"I know not. His words were…eager." A charming blush colored the older man's face. "Yet his manner was harsh. And—"

"Menacing," muttered Chardryn.

Dara nodded. "Savage."

"Joyful," Elina said. "When he looked upon my face, I saw—" What exactly had she seen in that brief widening of his eyes? "He was surprised. But also joyful."

"What I saw was more cunning. Or careful," the serjeant said. "At times they appear similar."

Elina would never regret a cunning or careful husband. "Perhaps he could not trust the joy he felt, and that explains the difference in his manner afterward."

"We waste our breath supposing and assuming. We will know what he feels if he follows," declared Chardryn, ever practical.

Elina sighed. Nanny Char was right, of course. It did no good to debate what Warrick would do and why he would do it, when the answer would come soon.

Though it could never be soon enough. The rising of the evening star seemed an eternity away.

A call sounded from the knights ahead—not unexpected, as they were soon to halt and make camp. Yet Serjeant Iarthil frowned and nudged his horse forward.

Dara poked her head out the carriage window opposite Elina's lounging pillows. She gasped. "He is here! The barbarian is here!"

He'd followed. Happiness surged through Elina's limbs, more powerful than any tonic. She sat up—too quickly. Her head spun. By the time the dizziness faded, the carriage had drawn to a stop. Her attendants all tumbled out.

Out of necessity and a burning desire not to fall flat on her face, Elina gripped the supporting hands of her porters and slowly descended the steps. A small gawking crowd had formed between her and the pool, yet they parted at her approach.

Her every thought seized to a halt when she spotted the figure in the turquoise water, just beyond the clouds of mist floating at the base of the third waterfall. It was a large pool, wider across than an arrow could fly. Shallow at the edges before abruptly deepening into an underwater ravine, the change in depth was marked by a darker blue and a visible current. Warrick stood at the edge of that ravine, the crystalline surface of the pool lapping at his abdomen. Droplets of mist clung to his sunbronzed skin, glittering over every visible inch of thick, wet muscle.

"Dear gods," breathed Nanny Char.

The corners of Serjeant Iarthil's lips twitched. "I suggested he bathe. It seems he listened."

Elina wished for a bath, too. Though hers would be in her tent.

But…why must it be?

Almost without thought, Elina began tugging the lacings at her waist. "Dara. Help me."

The maid tore her gaze from Warrick. Her fingers flew over the fastenings of Elina's robe.

The brocade dropped away. Instantly Elina's breathing eased. "I left my crown in the carriage, serjeant."

Chardryn belatedly realized Elina's intention. "Your Highness, you will catch a chill—"

"I daresay the day is warm enough, Nanny Char. As is the water." The gold underdress slithered down her legs. Dara held Elina's hand to steady her as she stepped out of it, leaving her clad only in her sandals and a lightweight shift made of white silk.

The old nurse shook her head. "A chill is not the only danger, my queen. You cannot swim."

"I will stay in the shallows with my betrothed husband."

"But the snakes and river beasts—"

"What will they do? They cannot harm me with their fangs or stings." Not while Elina wore her enchanted rings.

"What of—"

"Nurse Chardryn." The steel in Elina's voice sliced through the next protest. "I have not much time to live. So what little time I have left, I will seek what pleasures I can."

The old nurse's face softened. "Of course, my queen."

Elina accepted the support of Serjeant Iarthil's arm on her walk to the pool. Her heart pounded with every step, her gaze never leaving Warrick, who watched her come, his eyes narrowed against the sun. Water and muscle rippled when he lifted his arms to scrape a knife over his head, the gleaming blade cutting through thick tangles of hair.

Likely ridding himself of bloodsucking vermin—for which Elina was grateful. She did not wish to catch fleas and add itching to her daily list of pains.

She paused at the edge of the pool to remove her sandals. "I will be well on my own from here, Serjeant."

Bowing his head, he retreated one step. Though he did not say it, Elina knew he would stand there until she returned.

Gingerly she waded in. The water sloshed around her ankles, then her calves, deliciously cool. Rounded pebbles welcomed her soft feet. She caught a wavering glimpse of her reflection and stifled the sudden need to burst into hysterical tears or hysterical giggles. Or both. Her hair was still lovely, tall and powdered, but the queen's face had *horribly* melted. At least, melted everywhere that the mask hadn't dried into cracked patches of paint. Thickened globs of gold sagged beneath her eyes, around her nose and mouth. *And* he'd seen her puke.

But he'd still followed.

That thought chased away her hysteria. Water splashed around her knees and thighs as she moved deeper, wetting her shift, making the silk cling to her legs. She forged forward, up to her hips, her waist. All the while Elina searched his eyes for even a hint of the joy that she'd seen before. His gaze remained narrowed. Watchful. Another swath of tangled hair fell from his head and was gently pulled toward the center of the pool by the current at the ravine's edge.

The effort of wading through the water rendered her breathless when she finally stood before him, though the wonderful buoyancy made standing no effort at all. Water that was waist-deep to Warrick came up to the tips of Elina's breasts, and she suspected the splashing had rendered the silk fully transparent. Yet she could not spare even a glance at herself. Not when Warrick stood before her and looking at him was such a sweet pleasure.

And there was so *much* of him to see. But her eyes were drawn first below the water—to a rune on his hip glowing a steady gold. In the prison, the ragged wrap he'd tied around his waist had concealed the mark, yet she was unsurprised to see it.

She'd heard of such runes before. Those who were born in the Dead Lands, fearing a repeat of the Reckoning that had nearly destroyed the realm, voluntarily and permanently contained their innate magic within their skin. Those who were marked with the rune could not cast spells. Only a few witches born to the various clans retained that ability, and they only used spells for critical needs such as healing fatal wounds. But the mark also acted as a ward, making Warrick impervious to spells—so long as his innate magic was stronger than the sorcerer who cast the spell.

Which would serve him well in Aleron. His magic only needed to be stronger than her uncle's.

"May I touch you?" she whispered, her fingers poised inches from his skin. He could not understand her words but could probably interpret her tone and the hovering of her hand.

A single nod was his response. Even as she watched, his every muscle seemed to flex and harden, as if to steel himself against her touch.

Did he fear losing control? Did he want her so much?

She laid her palm over his heart. His *pounding* heart. Happiness bubbled through her veins at the evidence that her nearness affected him in equal measure to her own racing heart. Oh, and he was so warm. And smooth. In the cell, dirt and matted hair had covered his pectorals. Yet he'd shaved his torso. Even the dark trail arrowing down to his groin was gone. There was only bare skin beneath the water. And a thick—

Oh.

It was not as she expected. Elina had thought his appendage was supposed to stiffen when she came near. Yet hadn't she also overheard jests from the knights about how frigid water could shrivel a prick?

The pool must be too cold for it to harden—though to Elina, the water seemed only wonderfully refreshing. Certainly it had not cooled her own ardor. Or her blush. The heat in her cheeks would finish melting the queen's face if she looked any longer.

Averting her eyes from that fascinating hang of flesh, she let her palm slide across his chest, down his side. Her fingers dipped underwater. The glowing rune seemed hotter than the surrounding skin, though not burningly so.

She looked up. No tangled hair concealed his face from her now. His features were constructed of sharp edges, from the hardness of his jaw to the angles of his cheekbones. His eyes were dark, a brown so deep it was almost black, with a gaze that seemed to pierce straight through her.

"I am so very glad you came," she said softly. "Especially if it means that your heart is already mine."

His eyebrows drew in slightly, as if in confusion. Wondering what she was saying, perhaps. Elina was glad he didn't understand her. Never would she speak so freely if he could.

"I think I shall like having you in my bed."

His muscles went rigid. Had he heard the husky note in her voice? Was he stopping himself from ravishing her now? It was a lovely thought. Though perhaps not so lovely in practice. Not with every attendant watching.

Her gaze slid from his face. A tuft of hair stuck out above his ear. "You have missed there. May I?"

She gestured to the knife in his hand and was surprised by how tightly he gripped the handle. As if preparing to use the blade.

After a long moment, he seemed to understand her request and relinquished the knife. But he must not have understood her purpose—or that he was far too tall.

Elina crooked her finger. Stiffly, he bent his head.

Carefully she scraped away the tuft but saw that her task was not yet done. "There is more behind…"

Realizing the uselessness of explaining, she slipped around him. A few more tufts needed shaving—and he'd cut his scalp. A thin rivulet of blood flowed down the back of his neck, into the valley of his spine. Her gaze followed that crimson path, entranced by the two hollows dimpling the small of his back, just above the muscular swell of each buttock.

But all of this could be explored later. She returned her attention to the cut.

"My nurse can—"

Something seized her leg. Her gasp became a desperate gulping breath just before it pulled her under.

Don't panic, don't panic, don't panic.

Every lesson the serjeant had ever taught Elina about how to respond to an attack threatened to flee her brain, yet she hauled them back.

Fear might save her life. Panic would kill her.

Figure out what is happening. Are you hurt?

Rushing water swirled around her. Something was dragging her into the ravine but she wasn't hurt. She could feel the pointed pressure of the teeth around her ankle, but no pain. The jewels saved her from that harm.

Who attacked you? Do they have weapons or are they using magic? Are you in immediate danger or are they taking you somewhere?

Through the swirling water she caught a glimpse of

thick, pebbled skin. A long reptilian tail. Elongated jaws with rows of serrated teeth.

A mudbeast. She'd been taken by a snapping mudbeast. The kind that dragged their prey underwater to drown.

The realization forced her to beat back another surge of panic. The mudbeast was not hurting her…but she *would* drown. Her rings protected her from outer harm, not inner harm. Water in her lungs was most definitely inner.

And her chest was already aching so badly.

Do you have a weapon? Can you injure them?

Elina's entire body screamed as she curled forward, fighting against the flow of water, against the desperate need to take a breath. She might thrash forever trying to stab its undulating body with Warrick's knife, but she knew exactly where its brain was because its jaw was clamped around her foot.

Wildly she stabbed its head. Again and again. Either its skull was too thick or her arm was too weak.

She plunged the blade deep into its eye.

The mudbeast's head whipped to the side, jolting her hands away from the knife. Then the beast went still.

Dead.

Can you get safely away?

She couldn't swim. But perhaps she could shove her feet against the side of the ravine and push herself upward.

The beast's teeth were still clamped around her leg. Trying to pry its jaw open did nothing. Panic set in. She could remove the rings, rip open her ankle to get free—but the blood would only draw more mudbeasts to her and she would have no protection from their tearing jaws. Already she could see them, their circling shadows visible through the haze of glittering gold that hung in a cloud around her head. The paint and powder were washing off, leaving only the naked face of a woman who would never properly become queen.

She'd known she would die. But not this way. Not this way. When she'd only just found her warrior. When she hadn't freed her people.

Darkness filled the edges of her vision. A shadow approached—not circling but coming straight toward her. She would die here. But she would take another mudbeast with her.

With the last of her strength, she yanked the knife out of the beast's eye—and Warrick was suddenly there, just beyond the cloud of gold.

Too late. Her chest was about to burst, heaving relentlessly, her body fighting her mind in a frantic need to take a breath. She could not hold out long enough to reach the surface.

And Warrick—he did not appear frantic as he swam in closer. Or even concerned. Though grim, he seemed… pleased.

Surely that could not be. But whatever she'd seen in his expression mattered not at all when he suddenly stilled, staring at her. Perhaps memorizing her face as she was his.

Elina was not sorry that Warrick would be the last

thing she would ever see. And she could not fight her body anymore. Her last gasp exploded out of her lungs—

—and Warrick's mouth crashed down over her opening lips. She braced for the agony of drawing in water. But it was air. Hot, moist air.

Warrick had given her his breath.

Her chest still heaved for more. Yet the darkness receded.

His mouth broke away from hers and he vanished from her sight. The pressure on her ankle released. Then his arm circled her waist, small bubbles streaming around her as his powerful kicks drove them upward.

He shoved her up to the surface ahead of him. Elina broke through, coughing and gasping, into a cacophony of shouting and splashing. Serjeant Iarthil surfaced near them, relief scoring his face. Warrick swam with her toward the edge of the ravine, where it seemed her every attendant and knight was waiting to pull her into the shallows.

Warrick snarled at them all and swept Elina up into his arms.

She clung to his neck, still coughing, her lungs spasming painfully with every drawn breath. Her attendants swarmed around them as Warrick strode to the shore, where Nanny Char waited, her lined face made haggard by her concern.

"Let me have her. Let me tend to her. Serjeant Iarthil! Tell him!"

From behind Warrick, the serjeant said something in

the eastern tongue. Likely imploring the warrior to give Elina over into their care.

Warrick ignored them, sitting Elina upon one of the boulders surrounding the pool. He took her robe from a dripping Dara and wrapped the brocade securely around her shoulders—the heavy material no longer a smothering weight but a comforting warmth.

Elina had preferred his arms, yet could not say so while still coughing.

Someone thrust her underdress into his hands. Without hesitation he ripped the gold silk, then used a strip to tenderly wipe the water and the remains of the paint from Elina's face. His eyes followed every movement of his fingers, his expression caught somewhere between confusion and anguish.

Was he blaming himself? He ought not.

"I tha—" Another bout of coughing choked her gratitude into nothing before the constriction on her chest eased. She was finally able to gasp out, "I thank you."

His big palm cupped her jaw. He'd finished wiping her face, yet still he stared at her.

She sighed. "Not as lovely as the gold, I fear."

He frowned at the serjeant's translation. His thumb stroked her cheek as he rumbled his reply.

"He said that you are even more lovely."

She smiled against his hand. Then coughed into it, even as her body was wracked by a bone-deep shiver.

Chardryn hissed a worried breath. "Serjeant, we must

insist that the barbarian allows us to tend to her in the queen's tent. She *must* get dry."

This time Warrick nodded when the serjeant translated. Yet instead of giving way to her attendants, he picked Elina up with her shivering form swaddled in brocade.

The nurse bristled. "Warrior, give her over to one of—"

She broke off with a huff as Warrick strode past her, carrying Elina against his chest. Then she hurried after him, calling orders to the attendants. Elina's quarters had not been fully assembled before the uproar of the mudbeast's attack had sent everyone rushing to the pool, yet the tent was raised and her bed was within, though not yet draped with curtains.

Warrick set Elina on her feet. Serjeant Iarthil had followed them in, but spun to face away from her when Warrick stripped Elina of the brocade, then the shift. Dara appeared with a thick towel that he snagged out of her hands. Movements brisk, he set to drying Elina's naked form, holding her steady with one arm while he turned her this way and that, rubbing until her skin was tingling and pinkened by a combination of friction and embarrassment and pleasure.

When he crouched to dry her legs, Chardryn gave to her a warm honeyed draught to ease her cough and soothe her throat. Dara wrapped her wet hair to stop the water from dripping down her back. Warrick rose and turned Elina again—then paused, his towel hovering between her shoulder blades.

Elina had never seen the symbol that was etched there, though Chardryn had described it to her.

"It is the mark of a curse," Elina said, her voice raw with emotion. "A wasting disease that will soon kill me."

And telling him made her chest ache worse than nearly drowning had. Not until this moment, as his fingers traced the mark, had Elina realized how selfish she was. She'd only thought of her own happiness, the joy of knowing love, even if for only a short time. But if Warrick came to love her, only to watch her die…?

For so long, her barbarian warrior had only existed as a possibility, without a name or a face or any life outside of a role the prophecy said he would fulfill. Yet he stood before her now, a man of flesh and blood. A man who could be hurt.

Her breath hitched painfully in her throat. "I am so sorry, Warrick."

He tilted her head so that she looked up at him. His dark eyes searched hers.

"It was not…kind to ask this of you." She lifted her trembling hand to his face as Serjeant Iarthil translated. "It was selfishly done."

Warrick caught her fingers, pressed them to his lips as he spoke his reply.

"He says you asked nothing of him that he is not willing to do."

Elina could hardly speak after that. Was this how a spark of love began? With a bit of kindness and generosity that made her heart ache—and at the same time feel lighter than it had ever been?

She found her voice again when Dara approached carrying a nightdress. With a smile at Warrick, Elina said, "I see that Nurse Chardryn has given her orders. I will be commanded to nap, then confined to my bed for supper. Will you eat with me when I awaken?"

Warrick nodded after receiving the translation, then lowered her onto the bed, where Chardryn quickly tucked her beneath a blanket. Sleepily Elina thanked them. Nanny Char turned away to busy herself elsewhere, but Warrick remained standing at her bedside. Watching her. Perhaps waiting for her to sleep. She watched him in return through the drowsy fall of her eyelashes, and saw that his confusion and anguish had transformed into steely resolve.

What had he decided upon? Perhaps she would ask him. Later. When she wasn't *so* very tired.

Elina closed her eyes and slept.

WARRICK

the

OVERTURNED

The Falls

WHEN THE QUEEN'S EYES CLOSED IN SLEEP, WARRICK strode out of the tent—then stopped in disbelief. The sun was still high. The waterfalls still churned up mist. The river still flowed and the air still smelled of flowers. Everything was the same as when he'd gone in.

Yet nothing was the same. And everything was all wrong. *He* had been wrong.

Warrick had only dived in after the queen to retrieve the Stars of Anhera—thinking the gods had favored him by making his task so easy. When pondering ways to kill her, Warrick had not even considered a quick drowning.

When he'd come upon her at the bottom of the ravine,

she still lived, but was in the final battle against the need to breathe. He'd only moved in closer so he could watch her die in a cloud of gold, wearing the stolen jewels that had brought her to such a fitting end: caught in a cold-blooded reptile's jaws, trapped by the same power that ought to have kept her from harm.

Then she'd looked at him. And upon her face was such overwhelming despair and longing that it had taken Warrick a stunned moment to realize that she wasn't as old as he'd believed. That she'd likely been little more than a child when the jewels were stolen.

And her eyes. They weren't rheumy or clouded as they'd appeared in the prison, merely a pale gray. Almost silver. Yet still an old woman's.

What had she suffered to have eyes like that?

Whatever it had been, he would not let her suffer any more. Almost without thought—yet it had been a clear choice, made with his heart as much as his head—Warrick had fastened his mouth to hers, determined to save her even if he had to give his last breath to do it.

And the taste of her lips…

It had been wrong. All wrong. *Everything* was wrong.

A throat cleared behind him. "Did you not have enough gold to purchase clothes?" Iarthil asked.

Because Warrick had gone into the pool naked and carried Elina out the same way. Now he stood bare-assed in front of her tent, trying to understand how he'd been so thoroughly upended.

The serjeant might have answers for him.

"They are with my horse. Walk with me." Warrick started downriver, where he'd tethered his new mount. "Who cursed her?"

Iarthil fell in beside him. "Her uncle. Soren."

"He is a spellcaster?" Carelessly using corrupted magic.

"He is. Though I don't know if the curse is of his magic or if he paid another to do it. That has been his method these past ten years—though usually he only sends assassins after her, not sorcerers. Perhaps he did because the assassins always fail."

The last was said with an unmistakable note of satisfaction. "Because of you?"

"It is my sworn duty to keep her safe." That modest reply was followed by a hesitation. Then, "You will not remain king after the curse takes her. Aleron's throne is inherited through the female line, so when you've killed Soren and all is returned to what it should be, next upon the throne will be a female cousin. Though a distant cousin, as Soren killed all nearer female relations, including Her Highness's mother." His voice faltered. "It was over my queen's deathbed that I made a vow to protect her daughter—but I cannot protect her from this cursed illness."

Pain was clear upon the man's face, yet Warrick knew not whether his grief was for the queen—mother or daughter—or the grief of failing to fulfill his vow. He only said, "I have no wish to be king." Unless he was at her side. "When was she cursed?"

"Five years past. Two winters ago, we believed she was near the end. Then she received the jewels—the enchanted rings that kept the beast from harming her leg," he explained, fortunately, as Warrick had forgotten that he was not supposed to know what Anhera's stars could do—and his attention had been caught by another part of the explanation.

"She *received* the jewels? From whom?" From the fiend who'd stolen them?

When Iarthil seemed to struggle over how to answer, Warrick assumed he would lie. But apparently the serjeant only thought he wouldn't be believed. "A raven. It flew into her tent and dropped them into her lap."

"A *raven* gave them to her?"

"Many of us saw it," Iarthil said, looking offended that his own word might not be enough.

Warrick's disbelief was not that it had happened, but because the raven was Anhera's favored bird. Had the goddess herself made certain that the queen received the jewels?

Why? "Are they are keeping her alive?"

"They are. But she is declining again."

Not because of any curse. Yet Warrick said nothing. He knew not whom to trust.

Iarthil blinked twice when Warrick's new mount came into view behind a cluster of trees. "That is a monster of a horse."

Warrick grunted his agreement. But he could not have

purchased any other—he was no small man, so he could ride no small horse.

As Warrick belted a simple leather wrap around his waist and dragged on his boots, Iarthil examined his axe. Warrick had fastened to the weapon a new short handle and the long chain at a blacksmith's forge in Torrath.

At the prison, the queen had commanded Iarthil to tell Warrick about a prophecy in which a barbarian warrior killed her uncle with his axe, yet the serjeant had said nothing of a prophecy in his translation. Only that she needed Warrick to kill a usurper. Then he'd insisted Warrick bring the axe without saying why—and Warrick could not ask Iarthil about his reasons without revealing how much he'd understood.

Nor would he reveal that anytime soon. Better that everyone who surrounded the queen believed they could speak freely around him.

"Have you practiced swinging the axe by the chain?"

"I intend to now." Especially as Warrick was meant to kill her uncle with the weapon. "What is her name?"

"Elina." Iarthil regarded him steadily. "She is determined to have you. In that, I won't interfere. But do not harm her, or I *will* kill you."

"Fair enough. But fear not. You made a vow to your queen to protect her. I will make the same vow to mine."

Confusion furrowed his brow. "Your queen?"

Warrick glanced back at the Radiant Queen's tent, where the woman who'd overturned his entire world slept. "Elina."

• • •

Elina did not awaken for supper.

Two women were in the tent watching over her—one the maid who'd given to Warrick the robe at the pool and had helped him dry her. Dara, he'd heard her called. Along with the nurse, she seemed to be Elina's primary attendant. The other woman he'd seen in the gaggle of retainers who'd flocked into the pool to help save Elina, but knew not her name.

It was Dara who approached him as he stood by Elina's bed. She hadn't moved since he'd lain her down, not even to turn onto her side. Sleeping far more deeply than a mere nap suggested.

"Nurse gave to her a sleeping tonic with the draught for her cough. She won't wake again this night," Dara said—then attempted to say the same by pillowing her cheek on her folded hands and miming sleep, before shrugging and shaking her head.

Warrick nodded.

The other woman arched her brow at Dara, pursing her lips in clear disapproval—though unspoken disapproval. For the moment.

Warrick left the tent, then waited. The tent walls were no impediment to the voices within.

It did not take long. "Will you be tale-telling on Nanny, then?"

"I will not," Dara said sharply. "But the queen would

not be pleased about the draught. She wished to sup with him.”

“Nanny’s care will be the only reason the queen reaches home. If she ever does.”

“Whether she returns home or not, I should like to see her happy.”

“Oh yes, *happy*.” The woman gave a bitter little laugh. “I suppose at least one of our number should be. We have been apart from our families for a decade, but by all means—let us risk the queen’s health so she can be kissed.”

“Return to your family now, then. The queen will not begrudge your leaving, just as she has not the others who went. Though you know what happened to them when they arrived.”

By the other woman’s silence, Warrick assumed that they had not survived their homecoming.

An assumption confirmed when Dara continued, “What Soren did to them will happen to you. Our only hope of returning home is by staying loyal to her—or to her barbarian, if it truly is his axe that will fell Soren. So by the gods, I *pray* they kiss. And I pray he loves her enough to avenge her death and kill the king who cursed her.”

A deep sigh floated from the tent. When the woman spoke again, the bitterness was gone and her voice wistful. “Does he truly love her, you think? So quickly?”

“That is what the prophecy said. ‘From the first moment he lays eyes upon her face.’ And he’s here, isn’t he?”

Warrick was too thunderstruck to attend to any reply.

Something *had* happened within him when he'd first laid eyes upon Elina's face. Her true face, beneath the haggard paint. He knew not if it was love. Yet he *would* kill her uncle. And never would he abandon her.

Nor would he let Elina leave him. Not in death. Not by any illness. It was clear to Warrick that there was far more—and far less—to her uncle's curse than Elina knew.

But he need not ponder what it meant that a raven had delivered the Stars of Anhera to Elina, keeping her alive until she arrived in Torrath, where Bannin and Warrick had only remained long enough to meet her because Warrick had spoken to a dead man whose family was enslaved by Lord Gleris—a family who needed help to return home. Just as Elina's people wished to do.

Whether a prophecy or a goddess put him at Elina's side—or whether it had come about by chance—it hardly mattered. This was where Warrick wished to be.

Because until the moment he'd laid eyes upon her face, everything Warrick had thought and done had wronged her.

Now it was time to do what was right.

Elina began to stir not long after sunrise. She shifted toward Warrick with a soft sigh—the first time she'd moved since the previous day.

Whereas he had barely closed his eyes. It seemed that now he'd laid eyes upon her face, he couldn't look away. Almost the full night he'd spent watching her sleep, studying her every feature. But that had been in darkness and shadow. Now sunlight was filtering through the filmy bed curtains, and he was seeing her anew.

Her hair was still in its toweling wrap, but from the curling wisps that had escaped, he could see that it was a deep brown that glinted red where the light touched it. Her eyebrows were the same dark color, heavy slashes with the faintest arch. Long, thick lashes fanned across her upper cheeks, which were dotted with freckles. Her nose was pert, her lips soft—and she had a stubborn chin that he liked very well.

Altogether a pretty—if unremarkable—face.

His gaze returned to her eyebrows. Unremarkable, aside from those. In the prison, with her expression stiff under the paint, he'd hardly noted them. Yet after the pool, when her face was cleaned, her brows seemed to emphasize her every word—and sometimes they conveyed her thoughts so clearly that she needed no words at all.

Even now, while still half asleep, her brows had drawn in slightly—as if in puzzlement. Likely she had never before awakened with an aroused barbarian pressed full-length against her side.

Never again would she awaken without one.

Her silver eyes fluttered open. Those were remarkable, too. As was her mouth, when her slow smile transformed her lips into the most tempting lips Warrick had ever seen.

"You are here," she breathed.

"Good morn to you." And he would give a greeting that needed no translation. Gaze fixed on her lips, he lowered his head.

"Oh!" She slapped her palm over her mouth and turned her face away. Muffled behind her fingers, she said, "Chardryn's draughts make my mouth sour."

Warrick hardly cared. He wished to taste her again—to see if what he suspected of her illness was true.

But that was not the only reason he had to kiss her.

Angling his head, he feathered his lips over her ear and was rewarded when she gasped. She shivered as his mouth moved downward and he nipped the tendon at the side of her neck. Beneath the sheet, his palm slipped up over her ribs to cup her heaving breast through the silk of her nightdress.

Her breathing halted. Her body trembled.

Warrick stopped. "Elina?"

She turned her head, silver eyes meeting his. A blush stained her cheeks. Her soft bottom lip was pinched between her teeth.

Gently he swept his thumb over the swell of her breast. "It is all right that I touch you?"

No need to translate. She responded with an eager nod.

"Please," she whispered, her flush deepening. "I know nothing of how to do this. But whatever you like, it is what I wish."

Warrick would like to do everything with her. And they would have time enough.

He hooked his fingers into the neckline of her nightdress. Her gaze fell to his hand as he tugged the silk down over her small breast, revealing a dusky nipple that had already stiffened in anticipation of his touch.

Or his mouth.

She gasped again when he captured that tight bud between his lips, her body curling forward, her hands clutching at his head. Then she moaned softly, and settled back against the pillows, her eyes closed. Her breaths panted through her parted lips.

And the gods help him, the sweetness of her. Not upon his tongue, for that was just skin. Instead her sweetness was in his blood, with her every moan as he pinched and sucked, and with the way her hands caressed his head as if she needed to touch him in return, and how she stifled a cry and arched her breast toward his mouth when he lifted his head to see how rosy and swollen her nipple had become.

So beautiful. And so very sweet.

Hungrily he tugged down the other side of her nightdress—then glanced up to find her eyes awash in tears. His heart constricted.

Had he hurt her with his need?

"Elina," he said thickly.

She shook her head, giving him a tremulous smile. "Ignore my tears. I am happy. It seems that everything I do is accompanied by pain. But not this. Not with you."

"Never with me," he vowed. "And I will see your pain end."

Her hand slipped down to cup the side of his face.

"You will have to tell me that again when we are with Serjeant Iarthil. I am certain I will like what you said."

"Good morn, Queen Elina!" Light flooded the bed as the curtains were thrown back. Warrick reached for his axe—and stopped at a startled squawk. "Forgive me, Your Highness!"

The curtains were yanked closed.

Elina began shaking with laughter, sputtering into her hands. Then she sat up, pulling her gown back into place while giving him a look of regret. "I suppose I need my tooth powders before we can do much more, anyway."

Warrick would have been happy to show her much could be done without kissing. But he would be patient.

He sat back against the pillows as the curtains opened again on Elina's side of the bed. Dara, holding a tray heaped with fruit and toasted bread.

The curtains next to Warrick swept open. A small cup in hand, the nurse announced, "Your tonic, my— May the gods help you, girl! You'll never survive *that*!"

Horror overspread the older woman's face. She—and now Elina and Dara—stared at the sheet covering Warrick's cock, where the silk had pulled tight enough to show the length and thickness of his erection.

Elina snorted, breaking the stunned silence. Then all the women burst into laughter, the nurse and maid doubling over to support themselves against the mattress.

"Oh! Oh, I've spilled the—" Holding her side, the nurse backed away. "I have to mix up a new..."

Her voice trailed off as she left the tent. Dara wiped her eyes and arranged the tray in front of Elina. "I was about to say, there is more substantial fare for the…" She faltered as she looked to Warrick, uncertain what to call him.

"My betrothed husband."

"For your betrothed husband. Eggs and meats and such. But we were afeared the smell would turn your stomach, so I didn't bring them in."

"I thank you, Dara. Ask the serjeant to attend us shortly; he can convey that to my warrior then. See that enough breakfast is saved each day. By the look of him, he'll eat a hefty amount."

"Indeed, Your Highness." With another quick glance at Warrick's lap, Dara retreated.

Grinning, Elina reached for the toast. Warrick sat up, plucked a fat raspberry from the bowl and brought it to her lips.

"Oh." Her eyes locked on his as she obediently opened her mouth. He slipped the berry in and followed with a kiss, gently, pressing his open lips to hers. The barest graze of his tongue along her inner bottom lip could not tell him what he needed to know, the flavor of raspberry was so sharp and strong—but he cared not at all. Because that small lick made Elina moan low in her throat, and she clutched at his shoulders, smashing her toast against his skin. Gently he coaxed her to open a little wider, sliding his tongue between her teeth to tease the tip of hers.

Eagerly she responded, and her lips were swollen and her expression dazed when Warrick finally pulled back.

Then he selected another berry and went in for more. "Your tonic— Oh!"

Elina laughed against his mouth before turning toward the nurse. "It is well, Chardryn. Though in future mornings, I will call for you when I am ready to leave my bed."

Taking the small cup, Elina drank the contents in one swallow. Chardryn bustled away again.

Warrick reached for another berry, then paused. Elina had squeezed her eyes shut. Her breathing was quick and shallow, her face pale.

"Elina?"

"I am well. I just…I do not think I can manage breakfast. Or more kissing. Nor can I bear to puke in front of you again. Or *on* you."

Her wry smile couldn't conceal her regret and embarrassment. Warrick stroked a thumb down her cheek.

"You may do anything you wish to me, Elina."

"I only understood my name, but I like how you say it very much."

Her sweetness filled him again and he reached for the raspberries—taking the full bowl, not just one. "I will bring these along with me. All day, I will remember the taste of your mouth and the feel of your nipple against my tongue."

She might not have understood a word, but she didn't misinterpret his tone or the look he gave to her lips. A blush overspread her cheeks again.

Satisfied, Warrick swept the sheet aside and left the bed. He collected his leather wrap but did not yet bother to put it on. In the corner of the tent, attendants were filling a bathing tub. Not big enough to share. He strode out into the early morning sun and a burst of giggles sounded from the attendants inside.

Dara approached carrying a pail of steaming water. She mimed shoveling food into her mouth and pointed.

"My thanks."

Her cheeks pink, she smiled and bobbed a curtsy before sweeping past him. A moment later, another burst of giggles came from Elina's tent.

Serjeant Iarthil came upon him next, brows raised high and eyes dancing with laughter. "Even in the Dead Lands, I believe warriors wear their clothing instead of carrying it."

"Not before a morning's bath." Elina was sensitive to smells. So he would make certain she was not repelled by his.

Understanding dawned on the man's face. "Well done. Have you eaten?"

Not enough. He followed Dara's direction and the wafting scent of roasted meats to a tent under which stood three tables laden with platters. Over thirty knights and attendants shared the benches—a number which didn't include those who were on duty. Ignoring the plate offered, Warrick chose a whole leg of lamb, and carried it to the pool. He ate the meat off the bone while standing naked in the water, letting his mind toss through everything he'd heard and seen since Elina appeared at the prison. Envisioning the path forward.

Everyone thought him a barbarian with strange ways. And so he was, in truth. Yet few outside of the Dead Lands knew anything of the clans aside from rumor and legends.

Warrick would put that ignorance to use.

He was briefly surprised that Elina did not again wear an ornate costume. But he'd believed her an arrogant monstrosity then, coming to a prison garbed in gold. Now he saw the ceremonial aspect for what it was—and realized that even the words of her haughty proposal had likely been traditional.

He also now understood how tightly Elina had clung to the little strength she had just to rise from her chair and stand before him in that heavy crown and robe. How she'd fought to simply speak the words without retching from the stench of his cell.

The day before, he'd despised her. Now Warrick could do nothing but admire her. His strength had always come easily. He'd never had to fight his own body's weakness. Yet Elina did each day.

At least her clothing on this day would not weigh her down. In a wisp of a gown that skimmed her slender curves from shoulders to mid-thigh, she stood with Iarthil—both of them looking at a large parchment overspread on a table.

A map. Serjeant Iarthil glanced up as Warrick joined them. "We travel north to Darcoth. In that city is a temple of Khides—you will be married by the priestess there."

"Vows can be spoken anywhere."

"Not if you are the Radiant Queen," said Iarthil. "We should arrive in Darcoth by Midsummer Eve. Your ceremony will take place on Midsummer Day, so that every citizen of Aleron—whether in the kingdom or abroad—will be taking part in festivities on the day of our queen's wedding. Then we will return to Aleron."

Warrick found that kingdom on the map. His heart leapt against his ribs. The shortest route would take them west through Galoth—and the Stars of Anhera would come with them.

The jewels were keeping Elina alive now. But he would discover the root of her cursed illness so that she would no longer need them.

And if he did not…

Warrick's throat tightened. He would not think of that. Such a choice could not be made. And so by the time they reached Galoth, Elina *would* be well enough that she no longer needed the jewels.

"Through Galoth and the Glass Mountains?" Warrick confirmed, tracing the route with his finger.

"Not west. We'll return on the roads by which we came." Iarthil indicated a route that trailed north and east.

Warrick frowned. "That is far longer."

"We've made allies and friends along the way. It will be safer for the queen than traveling west through unknown kingdoms."

A fair reason but an unnecessary one. "I have friends in Galoth who will see to our safety."

And after Elina returned the Stars of Anhera to them, every warrior in Galoth would likely march north by her side to help her take back her kingdom.

"Serjeant Iarthil." Elina was eyeing the man impatiently. "What does Warrick say?"

"He says that the route west is too dangerous to travel."

The words rolled smoothly from Iarthil's tongue. Not by a twitch did Warrick reveal that he understood them, though dread and fury abruptly roiled like molten lead within his chest.

Elina's face fell. "Is he certain?"

"He has been to Galoth. He says that in the wake of the stone sickness, bandits and warlords rule the roads. You would not be safe, even were there double the knights in your retinue."

With her finger, she longingly traced the western route. A resigned sigh escaped her. "And it is said the Glass Mountains are haunted."

"Quite full of ghosts," said Iarthil, smiling faintly. "Perhaps we might cut the distance through one of these routes." He tapped a northern road.

"It is still a long distance."

"Not *as* long."

She forced a smile. "Onward, then."

"Onward." Iarthil gave her hand a light squeeze, then rolled up the map. "We are ready to depart when you are, my queen."

Silently she nodded, her disappointment still clear upon her face. Warrick could say nothing. Fury burned in his chest.

Before this, he'd begun to think the serjeant was truly honorable. That Iarthil protected Elina was certain. Yet why take the longer road home if he believed she had not long to live? Would he not wish to return her to Aleron as quickly as possible?

And why had the man lied about his reason? What lay upon the road north that Iarthil wanted to revisit—or was there something along the western route he wished to avoid?

If the last, it mattered not. They *would* be going west. And without Serjeant Iarthil. Of that Warrick was certain.

But he could do nothing yet. Not until he rid Elina of her so-called curse.

His thunderous mood was not lightened by the slump of Elina's shoulders nor the weary, resigned way she regarded her carriage. At least *that* was something he could change now.

Warrick mounted his horse, then trotted the beast up beside Elina as she was being handed up into the carriage.

"Ride with me, Elina."

Instantly the nurse and attendants were all aflutter.

Warrick only cared for the yearning that filled Elina's eyes as she turned.

She darted a look at Iarthil. "Does he ask me to ride with him?"

Would the serjeant lie about this, too? Warrick held out his hand to her, making clear his invitation.

"Oh, but she cannot!" Chardryn cried. "She has not enough energy to ride!"

"If he holds me, I do not think I will need to expend any energy at all. And I cannot bear another hot day within that carriage."

"My queen—"

"When I tire, Nurse Chardryn, I will return to my pillows."

Elina reached up for his hand. Easily he lifted her slight weight, settling her sideways across his lap. Though the short length of her gown would allow her to ride astride, the saddle would chafe bare inner thighs—and Warrick had every intention of burying his head between those thighs when next he was in her bed. That would be no pleasure for her if her skin was tender and chapped.

With a happy sigh, she leaned back into the crook of his arm and rested her head upon his shoulder. Her sun-warmed hair had a pleasant blossomy scent that filled his every breath. "Tomorrow I will wear riding trousers."

And tonight she would wear nothing. But Warrick only grunted a reply. He could not respond to her here, when Iarthil might overhear and realize that Warrick understood what she said.

She lifted her head when he nudged his horse forward. "I feel as though I'm upon an elephant. This is the biggest horse I've ever seen. And, I'm sorry to say, the ugliest. Did they breed a troll to its dam?"

He could not stop his grin and buried his face against her hair, lest she see his reaction. Nor could he regret his near-laugh when Elina nestled in closer and splayed her hand over his heart.

All was quiet for a moment, then she gave a shaky little laugh. "Look at what you have done to me. Saving me. Kissing me. Holding me atop a troll of a horse. I'm so near to death. And yet…I feel as if I've finally begun to live."

So did Warrick. Beginning the moment he'd looked upon her face. His heart had been beating all these years, but he'd not truly known what it had been beating for.

He knew now. Just as he knew that Elina was *not* near to death.

But everyone who posed a danger to her was.

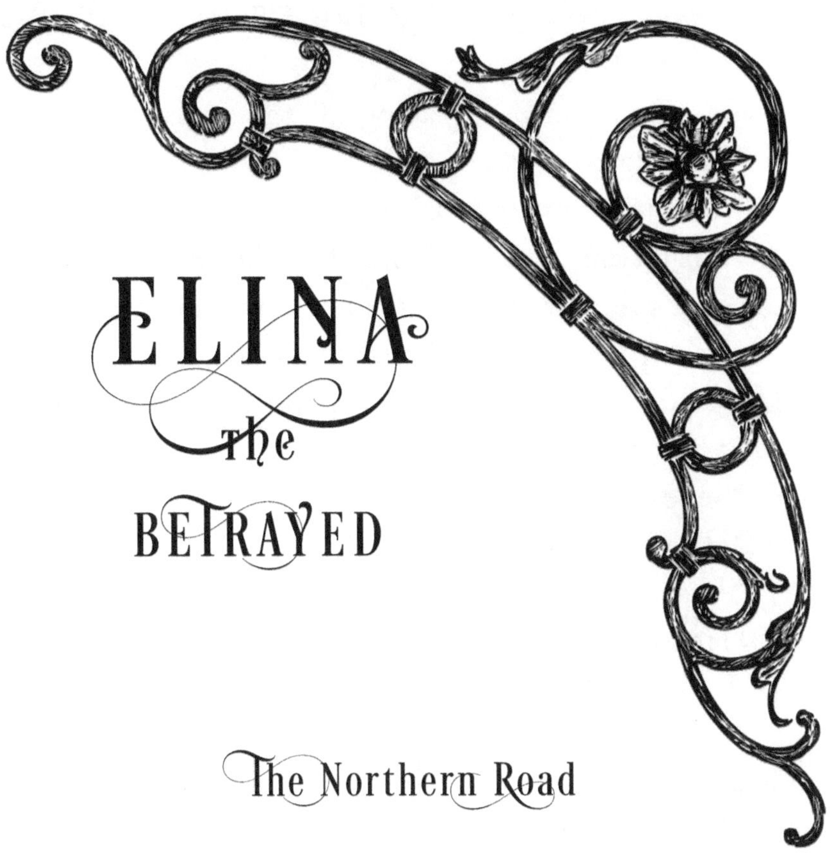

ELINA *the* BETRAYED

The Northern Road

Elina lasted until midmorning. She'd done well until suddenly the rhythm of the horse's gait had her leaning over and puking onto the ground. Through it all Warrick tenderly held her—though when he laid her in the carriage, his face was stone. Elina might have assumed that expression meant he was angry if she had not seen it so often in her mirror.

It *was* anger, of a sort—the rage of helplessness. Of being powerless to change a situation, for better or worse. That was a rage she knew too well.

He settled Elina onto her lounging bed and mounted his horse, but he did not go far. From her pillows, she could watch him riding alongside the carriage on that troll of a stallion.

"Your tonic, my queen."

"I thank you, Chardryn." Gratefully she sipped, savoring the cool sweetness that soothed her raw throat.

A sharp query from Warrick made her glance outside. His gaze was focused on her cup but Elina wasn't sure what he'd asked.

"Serjeant?"

"He asks what that is you drink."

"A tonic—to give to me energy and strength."

"He asks if it does."

Elina nodded.

Warrick's next response drew a small frown from the serjeant. "He says he will need to know how to make it."

"Ask him why."

Warrick's reply raised the serjeant's eyebrows. "He says it is a custom in the Dead Lands that, in the three days following marriage, a husband must see to his wife's every need. He prepares your food, your drink, your bath." His face reddened slightly. "He says that you will need no attendants. His will be the only face you see, his body your only covering."

Scowling, Chardyrn placed her hand on the lid of her apothecary chest as if to protect it from invading barbarians. "The tonic is no mere drink. Many of the powders are rare; some of the herbs cannot be procured anywhere nearby and are not easily replaced. And the measurements must be precise. Too much, and medicine becomes poison."

Serjeant Iarthil relayed her response to Warrick.

His confident answer needed no translation.

"My family has served the Radiant Queens for generations upon generations," Chardryn protested. "*I* have cared for Queen Elina since she was a babe. It is my duty to tend to her health, and no barbarian can possibly—"

"No one doubts your care for me, Nanny Char," Elina said gently. "But he will be my husband, my king consort, and we *will* respect his customs. You will show him how to mix the tonic…and after the wedding, I'm certain that he will allow you to oversee the use of your powders and approve the measurements when he makes the tonic for me."

Chardryn searched her eyes. "You trust him with your very life, Your Highness? A thief? The witch's prophecy might have meant another."

"With his own breath, he saved me," she said simply. "And he might be a thief—but what he stole, he set free."

The nurse huffed in response. But Elina knew that sound well. Chardryn had accepted her answer.

"Teach him to make it in these remaining days before the wedding." Elina leaned back against her pillows, smiling. "And if he botches the measurements or wastes the powders, I give to you permission to use your nanny's switch on his hand."

Happily Iarthil relayed that, though by Warrick's

grin he'd caught on to Elina's teasing tone before it was translated.

Oh, but her warrior was truly fine to look at. All that bare skin and muscle gleaming in the sun. Never had lying in the carriage been such a treat as now, when she could watch Warrick as they traveled.

He gave to her a look that seemed both hot and wicked before retrieving a pouch from the pack tied to his saddle. From it he plucked a red raspberry.

His eyes met hers as he brought it to his mouth.

Instantly she could taste his kiss, so tart and sweet. She could feel his lips at her breast. And the gods help her, his *tongue*. Just the barest lick had seemed to draw every inner part of her body into a hot, tight coil.

"Are you well, Your Highness? Your face has flushed."

"We must cool her down," Chardryn ordered. "Open the fans and stir up a breeze."

A breeze soon stirred. But since Warrick withdrew another berry from the pouch, cool air did not help her much.

"You added too much doxweed! Do you wish for hair to sprout from between the queen's toes? Oh, you thick-headed brute! Let us begin *again*."

In her tub, Elina hunched down deeper into the water, desperately holding back her giggles. Nanny Char was in the attendants' tent with Warrick, but much of her lesson could be heard from Elina's bath.

Dara's lips had compressed to pale strips. Elina met her eyes.

"Do you think she will use the switch?"

The maid sputtered out a laugh before catching herself. "Forgive me, Your Highness."

"What is there to forgive?" Elina had laughed, too.

"If I may say, you look very happy."

"You may say it all you like, because I am."

"I'm glad of it. Not just for Aleron. For you."

"I thank you, Dara."

They both turned their heads toward the front of the tent when Warrick came inside, carrying her tonic.

Chardryn was close on his heels. "You can't mix it up far in advance or it loses potency. So once you've added the water, bring it to the queen as soon as you can. Don't be off strutting naked through camp when that cup ought to be at her lips."

"Serjeant Iarthil is not here to tell him what you're saying," Dara reminded her.

"You should not be saying it at all," Elina added mildly. "You have much leeway with me, Nanny Char, for I am familiar with your manner and you used to change my diaper cloths. But even you should not make a habit of calling my king a thickheaded brute."

Chardryn flushed at the reproof. "Yes, my queen. Forgive me."

"All is forgiven." And was easily done. She arched a brow and lightened her tone. "Tell me, though—was he truly thickheaded?"

"Not at all, Your Highness. Though stubborn, for sure. He asked what everything was and what it did. Iarthil could open his own apothecary with what he learned talking between us. Go on now," she said with a nudge to Warrick, who had been standing motionless next to the tub, staring down into the bath—which hid nothing of Elina's nude form or how rosy the warmth of the water had turned her skin.

He knelt and gave to her the cup, his dark eyes never leaving her face as she drank it.

"I thank you." She handed the cup over to Dara and caressed Warrick's jaw with her wet hand. "I will be to bed shortly."

His gaze dropped to her mouth.

Elina arched a brow and tilted her head at the curtained bed.

With a rumbling growl low in his chest, he caught her lips in a hard kiss. He rose to his feet while she was still catching her breath—and if the bulge at the front of his leather wrap was any indication, Warrick was no less affected than she.

He started toward the bed, unbuckling the strap that held his axe to his back, then unfastened the belt at his waist. As he walked, his leather wrap dropped to the floor, where he left it.

Elina twisted around in the tub to watch him go. Dara's and Chardryn's eyes followed him, too, until he stepped through the filmy curtains. A lantern had not been lit within, yet the small amount of moonlight filtering through the tent walls offered to them his silhouette as he sat upon the bed.

A boot was tossed out through the curtains. Then the other.

Muttering something about barbarians, Chardryn collected the items and set them neatly aside, then settled on a cushioned stool next to the bath. Her concerned eyes slipped over Elina's face and settled on her lips, still reddened from his kiss. "Has he been gentle with you, girl? Has he frightened you or taken more than you wish?"

Elina doubted Warrick would ever take more than she would wish. Yet she did not think that was what Chardryn meant. "I am still a maid. He knows I must be a virgin at my wedding."

"You may still be a maid but he is still a barbarian. And the bizarre stories you hear…" She tutted and shook her head.

Dara winced. But her slight nod of agreement piqued Elina's curiosity.

"What bizarre stories?"

"Their unnatural practices," Dara said, then lowered her voice to a whisper. "In bed."

"Not only in the bed!" Chardryn interjected. "Anywhere they like! In the mud, up against walls, while riding horses."

While riding a horse? Had Warrick wished to while riding that morn—was that why he had invited her to share his saddle?

Oh, she could not wait until the ride tomorrow.

"And they do it as beasts do! Not face to face as the gods intended."

"Like horses, I've heard," Dara said.

"Or dogs," agreed Chardryn.

"And pigs?" Elina offered, for she had once seen a boar mount a sow.

A choking, snorting noise came from the bed. Immediately they hushed, glancing at each other guiltily. Then the guilt eased when Elina remembered Warrick couldn't have known what they said. She saw similar realizations on the others' faces.

"The noises men make." Chardryn grimaced. "And the smells. You'll have to get used to that now."

Elina could not count how many times over the years that Chardryn had fallen asleep in the carriage. Nothing Warrick emitted could be much worse than Nanny Char's snoring or farting when the window curtains were closed. But she nodded.

The nurse leaned in. "If he gets you on your hands and knees in the manner of a beast, insist that he turns you around proper. I once saw two dogs mating that way, and when the male got stuck inside the female—well, he just turned ass to ass and then dragged her down the street."

"Do you think that happens often in the Dead Lands?" Dara's eyes were wide.

"Be certain of it, child." She turned to Elina. "That

giant thing he's got will get stuck inside you for sure. Though once he spends his seed, it'll shrink fast enough."

No conversation had ever delighted Elina more. "So he won't be dragging me out of the tent, ass to ass."

"Oof! You never take anything seriously. But you'll see. Not just when he uses his big"—Chardryn wiggled her finger—"One can't help but hear the unnatural tales of how they kiss. How they nearly eat up the women they're with."

He'd certainly helped Elina eat the raspberry. "Do they only kiss with fruits, do you think? Or also cheese and meat?"

Chardryn looked utterly horrified. "That's not what I meant— Did he do that to you? Oh, you poor child."

Elina decided not to pursue that. "What *did* you mean?"

"That he'll kiss you everywhere. Not just your mouth."

Her breast, too. The memory pooled warmth deep within her belly and under the surface of her skin.

"*Everywhere*, child." Chardryn cast a significant look between her legs.

Elina pondered that, and the heat that rushed through her then was not merely warm, but blazing as she recalled the wetness between her thighs that morn, when she'd risen from bed after his kisses. And he wished to taste her *there*?

"Then it is very well that I'm taking a bath first," Elina concluded.

Dara chortled and pressed her hands to her red cheeks,

looking both delighted and scandalized.

Nanny Char clucked her tongue at Elina. "You're a bizarre one, too. Come now. Let us braid your hair and prepare you for bed."

Those preparations were too slow. And too fast.

Elina's heart seemed about to pound through her chest when they finally left her. Carrying a lantern might make her an easy target for an assassin's arrow—that had been a lesson learned years ago—so she made her way to the bed assisted only by the soft glow of the moon through the tent's walls.

Warrick waited for her, reclined against the pillows, his elbow cocked behind his head. The sheet draped across his middle from navel to mid-thigh. The massive bulk of his body seemed far too big for her bed, though it was of no small size.

And she was of no small heart. No small courage.

Chin high, Elina stripped the nightdress over her head and threw it aside.

Despite her boldness, a blush burned over every inch of her skin as she crawled in from the foot of the bed, feeling the dark gleam of his eyes upon her. He murmured something—Elina knew not what, but by the appreciative rumble, the husky edge of it, she thought he might have said she looked lovely again. Maybe not *only* lovely. Perhaps he'd also said delicious. So delicious he would eat her up.

And if he had not said that, she would pretend he did.

Instead of stretching out alongside him, she knelt at his right side and sat back on her heels.

Her fingers hovered over his pectoral. "May I?"

His big hand enfolded hers and brought it to his chest. Beneath her palm, his heart beat deep and steady…and steadily quickening. Elina could be in no doubt of his arousal. *That* she could easily see, though she was not brave enough to move the sheet. Not yet.

Instead she leaned forward, cupping his hard jaw, sliding her thumb over his firm lips. His head tilted back to meet hers when she bent down to kiss him. Softly, gently. Exploring the shape of his mouth with her lips, though she soon found it was an awkward position, with her arm braced beside his head to support the twist of her upper body over his.

His hand curved over her hip and nudged her closer. It took a moment to understand what he intended, for there *was* no closer. Unless she straddled him.

So she did, her lips never leaving his as her torso untwisted, as she was rendered breathless by the solid heat of his body between her thighs—or when she began laughing against his mouth.

A low rumble from his throat queried the reason.

She lifted away a few inches, shaking her head. But why not say? "It is only that Nanny Char and Dara said barbarians will do this *on* a horse, and do it *like* a horse—yet now I am astride as if *you* are the horse. And though it is true you are nearly as big as one, I am just glad you are not so ugly as yours."

His big hand clasped her nape and hauled her down for more kisses, peppering them over her face, her lips, her jaw, all the while his body shaking as if gripped by laughter. Perhaps he, too, had been diverted by a stray thought—or her amusement had sparked his. Whatever the reason, it faded soon enough. His mouth returned to her lips and his kiss deepened. The first slide of his tongue over hers sent her spinning into whirlpool of shuddering need, and continued until she couldn't think, couldn't breathe.

Near drowning in his kiss, she broke away, panting and trembling not only from his touch but from the effort of bracing herself above him.

She rested her forehead against his. "I wish I was stronger for you."

His hand smoothed up her side. His rumbling reply was reassuring, admiring.

She truly liked everything he said to her. Not a word did she understand but his meaning was clear.

So were his intentions when he rolled Elina onto her back. He rose over her trembling form, his thighs straddling her hips though he put none of his weight upon her. Then he kissed her again, not softly or gently but as if he hungered for the taste of her. As if she truly was delicious.

His warm hand cupped her breast and she gasped into his mouth. It was too much, his kiss *and* his touch.

Then he teased her nipple with his thumb, pinching her sensitive flesh, and she could not stop the cry that escaped her. For an instant it crossed her mind that they might soon be set upon by any knights who heard that faint scream—until Warrick murmured against her mouth, as if approving her loud response. As if praising her for the pleasure she'd taken in his touch. After that, Elina could no longer care if her entire retinue piled into her tent to watch, so long as Warrick did not stop kissing her.

And he did not stop, though he abandoned her lips. But the kisses continued, down her throat to the center of her chest, teasing her skin with his tongue and teeth until she was shaking with need, and the need for more. For Warrick to taste her nipple as he had before. Then, wonderful man, he latched onto her breast with a suckling kiss that made her clutch his head and writhe with the exquisite pleasure of it.

How the wanton ache in her nipples took up a second residence between her thighs, she didn't know. Yet Warrick seemed to. Because he began kissing his way down her stomach as if he understood exactly where to go. His body slid farther down the bed, and it seemed the entire world spun around her when he urged her legs apart.

Oh gods. Everything they'd said was true.

But it wasn't bizarre. It was the most magnificent, incredible thing. His tongue, everywhere. Swirling and licking. He found a spot that made Elina bite her lips against another scream and then he teased and teased and teased. His hands gripped her ass, tilting her up for a deeper taste when she almost squirmed away, not wanted to stop but it was so much, too much, as if she were dying—oh she was, she was—but this was surely the best way to go.

Then his tongue slicked just right. The ecstasy burst from within to without, through her curling toes and arching back and all centered at his mouth. She screamed, and then it was done, she was dead.

Though still in bed. With Warrick tasting his way back up her quivering flesh, then rising onto his knees between her widespread thighs. Head lolled to the side, she watched enraptured as his fist wrapped around his engorged shaft. He stroked, hard, fast, his dark gaze locked upon her face. It seemed only seconds passed before he grunted, his every muscle clenching. Seed spurted onto her belly in hot jets.

Chest heaving, he smeared his fingers through his spend, as if writing a rune onto her skin. He spoke, his voice low and so deep. So resolute.

A vow. Or a promise. It could not be a spell.

In the dark, the rune etched over his hip gave off a steady golden glow that lit his surrounding skin. Languidly she reached for it, intending to feel its warmth. Warrick caught her hand and brought it to his mouth, kissing her fingertips.

That would do just as well. Elina did not care what she touched as long as she touched him.

Releasing her hand, he retrieved her discarded nightgown, using it to clean the seed from her belly. Then he slid into the bed, drawing up the sheet and pulling her close, her back to his chest. Somewhat like beasts, though they were on their sides, and nothing of this position felt unnatural. Instead she felt comforted. Protected, with the thrum of his heart against her back and his hand cupping her breast.

She clasped him even closer, the jewels on her fingers gleaming against his forearm. No one had ever held her in this way before. But then, when was the last time anyone had held her at all?

Lady Faraine had been the last, she realized after casting back through her memories. The night they'd fled Aleron.

Once, it had been a memory that comforted her. Now it was one she didn't care to revisit.

"I pray that I am not a fool for trusting you," Elina whispered. "Nearly everyone I've trusted has betrayed me."

Warrick turned her toward him, sliding her upward on the pillow until they were face to face. His eyes searched hers in the dark, as if trying to read her mood, her meaning. Elina was not sorry he couldn't understand her. That just made it easier to say. Easier to expose the greatest scars upon her heart. She could share them…but remain safe.

"When I was young, I had few playmates. But my uncle Soren was there. Every day. Talking with me, playing with me. My father and mother were always busy with political concerns. And I had tutors aplenty. But he taught me to have fun—and Nanny Char would give us *such* looks as we laughed and explored and got into so much trouble—yet the best, most harmless sort of trouble. For we were always in the mud, or using sticks as swords, or sneaking where we ought not to have snuck. I had the best of childhoods because of him." Her whisper hoarsened as her throat tightened. "So many times since, I've wondered—was he merely toying with me, befriending a child he always meant to kill? Was he hoping that when I became queen he would be a powerful advisor, but then decided that role wouldn't be enough? So he killed my mother and sent assassins after me. Then sent this curse, this slow and painful death. If he'd ever had any feelings for me at all, it would have been quick."

A tear slid over the bridge of her nose. Warrick made a noise low in his throat, his hand cupping her face, his thumb brushing the moisture away.

"Then my father. His marriage to my mother was only to strengthen ties between two kingdoms—Aleron and Tagdon. He was third in line, so not expected to inherit Tagdon's throne. Yet he *did* inherit it after the blue fever came, and though they were still married, they ruled from their separate kingdoms. When my mother was killed, he was in Tagdon. So it was there we fled first. *Of course* he would protect me and protect Aleron's throne—after all, his own daughter would hold it, and I was his heir in Tagdon, as well.

"It was only by the merest chance that Serjeant Iarthil

learned that my father had arranged for me to be sent back to Aleron. Back into my uncle's hands. Because my father had no wish to embroil Tagdon in another kingdom's squabbles, he said—and because he was already overwhelmed with ruling Tagdon and did not want to be at war. He has since remarried and sired another heir. So he has no use for me, and I suppose that he understood better than anyone how easily the first in line can die to make room for another behind." Hearing the bitterness that crept into her voice, Elina forced her thoughts away from her father. "So we fled Tagdon."

Warrick's thumb stroked her cheek. She'd probably said enough—or too much—but she couldn't stop.

"Then there was Lady Faraine." Her throat tightened into a clump merely saying the name. "She'd come with us when we first fled. She'd been my mother's lady-in-waiting, her friend, her closest advisor. And she promised my mother that she would help guide me through the courts we traveled to."

He wiped her tears again, and a little laugh escaped her.

"Despite her promise, I was not easily helped. I was angry and grieving and—and…*vengeful*. We were reliant upon other kingdoms for sanctuary and alliances, but I had no patience for their politics or their concerns. And they had sympathy for me but no one was willing to risk their armies to help a screaming child regain her throne. So Lady Faraine, she taught me how to speak at other courts, to control my anger. Taught me to be clever instead of rash. Taught me that when a situation makes me want to both laugh and cry, to choose the laughter. She continued the lessons my mother had begun—and she became to me as she was to my mother. A friend. An advisor. And I confided in her. Of course I confided in her—there was no one else. A queen cannot lay her burdens on her maids and attendants. But Lady Faraine, I could always speak with her. Of my rage and my grief. Of my hopes. She *knew* me, Warrick. Better than anyone. Better than my mother ever had, or even Soren had, because Lady Faraine and I were always together. For years, while traveling. Or… still fleeing, in truth. Soren had begun sending assassins after us. One even managed to—"

She turned to show Warrick the scar just below the ribs on her right side. His blunt fingertip traced the ragged puncture, then slipped around to her back where the arrow had poked through the other side.

"Elina." He growled her name and pulled her close into his chest. Struggling against more tears—though from the care he showed her rather than from the pain of her memories—she pressed her face into his throat. Her arm rose to wrap around his neck, clutching him to her.

Her breath shuddered against his skin. "The assassins always found us, so we rarely stayed anywhere for long. And in each kingdom we sought allies. Someone who might be willing to stand against my uncle. Always going farther and farther from home—and I had begun to suffer from a deep melancholy. The first heat of anger had passed, my mother was dead, my father indifferent to whether I lived. We had been gone for three years, and I was *so* tired, Warrick. And beginning to think that returning to Aleron and fighting my uncle was a hopeless cause. Until the witch. The witch that healed me when—"

She touched her side again.

"She spoke to me a prophecy. *'Bind to you with ribbon red a warrior who knows the weight of chains. From the Dead Lands he will come, and by his axe your tyrant will fall.'*" Elina paused. She would not say how she was supposed to know her warrior. Her heart was too vulnerable and Warrick's presence here too precious to speak it aloud now, as if it might conjure another warrior who would forever follow her after laying eyes upon her face. She wanted only this one—and his axe. "Truthfully, it says nothing of *you* killing my uncle. Only that your axe will. So I only need marry you and take your weapon. But I will take you as well."

A short chuckle rumbled through his throat in response to her teasing tone. She pulled back and found her lips caught in a kiss.

Then they were face to face again.

"For certain I will take you," she murmured. Long years spent in this tent had taught her how loudly she could speak without being overheard outside. "Never did I truly think that I might be…" *Loved.* But she would not say that fear aloud. "Never did I think that I might know such pleasure as you give to me. I have heard that I could do it myself but until you, there were always attendants in my tent. It was something Lady Faraine insisted upon. For my protection as well as to provide witnesses to my virtue. Because one day, I would marry. And the queen *must* be a maid."

As foolish as that tradition was. For it was only established to assuage the fears of potential king consorts who wanted to be certain their issue would inherit Aleron's throne. In Elina's mind, better to have a consort dedicated to the queen's pleasure and the mutual devotion of their hearts. For what better way to make certain she would not take a lover?

Elina had said as much once to Lady Faraine, who'd agreed. Though when the time came, Elina's preferences in a consort had not mattered at all. "I did not know then, but my marriage had become her only goal. When we heard that Kael the Conqueror was searching for a bride, we spent a full year traveling to his four kingdoms. For he matched the description of the warrior in the prophecy."

Warrick stiffened. He snarled something that she understood not at all—except in the midst of it, he repeated the name she'd spoken.

"You know Kael the Conqueror?"

She could not interpret his brief, steely answer but liked very well the sneering curl of his upper lip.

"Even before the prophecy, I had told Lady Faraine that someone such as Kael was the sort of warrior that I needed. Not someone tied to their own kingdoms—for when he killed Geofry the Child-Eater, he was not yet king—or who would refuse to embroil themselves in the conflict of another realm. So it seemed a destined match. But when we arrived, he was already wed."

Warrick scoffed and spat a few pithy words that held a note of challenge. As if he'd declared that if Kael and Elina had married, Warrick would have taken her from him.

The thought made her smile. "I was disappointed, but only on behalf of Aleron and my people. I had no feelings for him, and that held true during the winter we spent in Grimhold, his southern kingdom. No feelings for him, but for his wife…? Oh, I admired her so. And it was in Grimhold that I learned of true magic from Queen Anja. Of kindness and love as the most powerful of all magics. Sometimes I feel that my heart healed there. I was not so melancholy, at least—but we could not stay in her court. So we continued onward, but I had new hope. Because if the prophecy led me to Kael, perhaps it would lead me to someone else who could help me. I was so *eager* to continue onward.

"But Lady Faraine, she was…" *What?* Elina still didn't know. "I like to believe she was tired. That she was longing for home. That she wished to be settled instead of always searching. *Not* that she merely wished to be rid of me. Because in Winhelm, she secretly arranged a betrothal between me and the crown prince of that kingdom. I had refused to marry him, of course, because my intention was still to return to Aleron. But one night, after a feast when it seemed the toasts were never ending and I was dizzy from wine, I hardly knew what was happening before she had me standing up with the prince and a red ribbon around our hands. But I refused to say the vows and…and…"

Her voice broke. But Warrick was there, murmuring her name, kissing her lips.

Swallowing hard, Elina forced out the end. "We left her in Winhelm."

Eyes narrowing, he pulled back slightly to search her face. As if looking for what was still unsaid.

And there *was* much unsaid. Hoarsely she confessed, "Never have I told anyone what she— She is a liar. I could not bear if what she said was true. I could not bear it."

Holding her face between his hands, Warrick gently kissed her again.

She drew a shuddering breath against his lips. Her whisper was raw and thick. "She told me that before Serjeant Iarthil was sent to bring me to my mother's deathbed, he'd vowed to keep me safe. Which is what he vowed when I was there. But…Lady Faraine said the *first* vow that my mother made him swear was never to bring me back to Aleron. So that I would always be safe from my uncle. Because my mother feared I was not strong enough to defeat him." Her breath hitched. "Lady Faraine said that *my own mother* thought me too weak to hold Aleron's throne, so I might as well sit on Winhelm's next to an equally weak prince." She clutched Warrick closer, and closing her eyes did nothing to stop her streaming tears. "If true, my own mother had no faith in me. And Serjeant Iarthil has been leading me from place to place while only pretending we will return home. Keeping me safe, true. But not truly believing me queen of anything, with no true respect or care for me. Only duty, to a queen long dead. This, a man who I once wished was my own father—a better man than my father but no less false. But that is not all of it. That is not all."

Forcefully she stopped her sobbing breaths. But though her chest still hitched when she continued, her voice was flat. "Lady Faraine admitted that she had purchased the prophecy. That *she* had given it to the witch to recite. Because she'd known what I thought of Kael the Conqueror and had heard rumors of his bride search, so she paid the witch to give to me a prophecy designed to persuade me to marriage.

"I've said nothing of it to those who are still with me. To some, the prophecy had given hope, because we were all so tired. And I knew not whether there was anyone I could trust. I *do* trust Serjeant Iarthil to keep me safe, but do I trust that he will not undermine my intention to return to Aleron?" She shook her head. "So I trust no one. Which is so painful and lonely, Warrick. But everyone whom I've opened my heart to…it seems that once they've seen what is there inside me, they no longer think me worth their loyalty.

"But there was another reason I did not tell anyone

the prophecy was false." She swallowed hard against the ache in her throat. "In Grimhold, with Queen Anja, I learned that when wishes are spoken aloud, they sometimes become a spell—and that when something is said enough, it can become truth. And I so desperately wanted every part of the prophecy to be true. I wanted to find someone who would help me fell my uncle. Someone I could trust, because they would not care for me merely out of duty or because of a vow made to another queen—but because they had looked at me, and they'd seen someone worthy of their love and loyalty. I wanted to know what it is to be loved. *Truly* loved."

She sighed heavily, feeling completely emptied out. "And perhaps the prophecy has always been true. Lady Faraine might have lied about paying the witch. She might have been lying about all of it, so that I would lose faith in Serjeant Iarthil and give up my quest. But I could not be certain whether she lied or not. The truth seemed impossible to know. And after I was struck by my uncle's curse, it seemed all the more imperative to speak the prophecy into being. So that I could help my people… and maybe know a little of love before I die.

"So I never stopped speaking of it. Though I dared not hope it would come true. Until you. Now I pray that I am not wrong to open my heart to you, because I think another betrayal might kill me. If the curse does not do it first."

Elina laughed the last, because she was tired of

crying—then could laugh no more with Warrick's kiss fierce upon her lips. *So* fierce, and so deep, as if to persuade her that she was not wrong to open her heart. As if with this kiss, he vowed never to betray her.

Perhaps the meaning she felt in his kiss was only a reflection of her own wish, but Elina wanted to let herself believe in it. He spoke her name against her mouth, then turned her again, her back to his chest, and held her securely in his arms. Almost like beasts again…and never had she felt so warm and protected.

Perhaps she *could* let herself trust again.

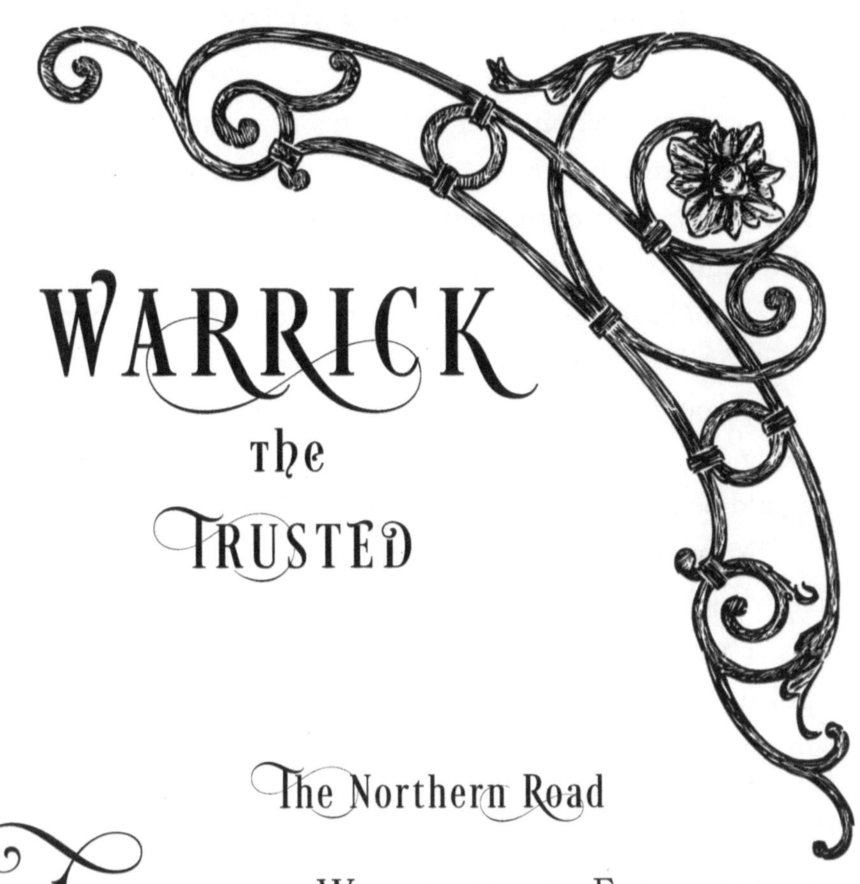

WARRICK the TRUSTED

The Northern Road

I**N THE MORNING, WARRICK GAVE TO ELINA A CUP OF** poison.

Or so it would seem to whoever had filled a jar of doxweed with bloodbane. The powders looked similar, but Warrick knew their smell and flavor—and despite Chardryn's careful labelling, the contents were *not* doxweed.

And it wasn't a curse that was killing Elina.

From the moment Warrick had given her his own breath, he'd suspected bloodbane from the taste of Elina's mouth—but there was always something to prevent certainty. Her tooth powders. The raspberry. The sweetness of the tonic.

But he was certain after tasting her cunt. Her body was steeped in the poison, its presence betrayed by the faint bitterness of an unripened cherry. So much bloodbane, she ought to have been dead.

Would have been dead, if not for the Stars of Anhera.

I think another betrayal might kill me.

It would not. Elina was strong enough to survive anything. Of that, Warrick was certain. But her heartbreak would become far worse before it was better.

So would her illness. Because even as bloodbane slowly killed, the flesh came to depend upon its presence. Its cessation and the purge were more painful than the poison…and Elina had so much bloodbane to purge, she might wish that a curse had killed her instead.

But the jewels would help her.

So would Warrick.

There were a few days yet, however, before the purge would begin. In that time, he could help her by finding out *who* had changed the powders.

Nurse Chardryn seemed the clear choice, for she carefully guarded her apothecary chest and monitored the contents. But anyone in Elina's retinue could have found an opportunity—particularly the maids and attendants.

In truth, after Elina had ripped out his heart with her tears and her story—and knowing that she would soon learn that Iarthil had betrayed her, as had whoever "cursed" her—Warrick was tempted to simply kill them all.

But that would not be the right thing to do. Surely

at least a few of them were still loyal to her. He would not kill innocents.

So for now, the right thing was to prepare the tonic under Chardryn's watchful eyes, but use a bit of thieves' trickery to make certain the bloodbane was never added to the cup.

"Warrick?"

Elina. He glanced through the carriage window. She reclined inside after sharing a saddle with him that morning. They'd both been quiet during the ride—Warrick brooding, and Elina almost shy with him, though whether that was a result of the cunt licking or her confession, he didn't know. Yet now her brows were arched high and her voice betrayed a note of alarm.

She gestured to his chest. "You're, uh…*glowing*."

That announcement was followed by every attendant within the carriage crowding Elina's side to look at the golden glyph that covered much of his torso and the upper part of his right arm.

Warrick had no need to look. He'd seen it many times before. "When did it start?"

"He asks when it began glowing," said Iarthil, riding up beside him.

"It began just now," she said with a smile curving her lips. "I like to watch him. So I have been for a while."

Warrick held back his grin until the serjeant translated her answer.

She grinned back. "Ask him what the glow means,"

she said and Iarthil did.

"That a ghost is nearby. Likely ahead of us, as I only just now came near enough for the archer to glow." Warrick gestured to the glyph, which resembled a bow and a quiver of arrows. "That means we've entered its haunt. So I will speak to it when I see it."

Iarthil stared at him. "A ghost?"

"As I said."

"Is the queen safe from it?"

"She is." Warrick impaled him with a look. "She will *always* be safe with me."

"Serjeant?"

Iarthil turned to Elina and spread his hands, as if to convey that he was trying to translate something that was beyond his ken. "He sees ghosts. We're in a haunt. He'll talk to it. We're safe."

Now Elina stared at Warrick. "Can *we* see it?"

Of course that would be what she asked. When Iarthil translated, Warrick held out his hand to her. "You can if you are touching me. Come." To the serjeant he said, "Tell her it might be gruesome."

"I will bear it," was her reply, and she clambered nearer to the window. Warrick pulled her through and onto his lap before urging Troll into a canter. Iarthil followed, along with a half dozen knights.

"Ohhh," she breathed, her gaze sweeping either side of the road, where shriveled trees stood over rotting vegetation and moldy soil. "I have seen blights like this before. I was told it was because of insects—or a disease that killed everything. But it is a haunt?"

Mayhap some blights were caused by those things. This one was not.

He gestured ahead, where a bridge crossed a sluggish brown river. In the summer's heat, the water had retreated from the banks, which were thick with mud.

Elina's breath caught. Her fingers spasmed on his arm. "I *see* her."

A woman, her hair white—though that was true for all ghosts. Mud was packed into her eyes and the gaping hole of her nose. Bilious green skin sagged in sheets from bony limbs.

The ghost stood on the muddied bank, downstream of the river crossing. He guided Troll onto the bridge, where Warrick could easily look at her and be seen in return. Dropping the eastern tongue, he spoke in the language of home. Ghosts always understood him, though Warrick couldn't always understand them. Yet he'd learned enough languages that he could converse with most.

"I see you," he said. "Who has wronged you?"

Mud fell in thick glops from the woman's opening mouth. Elina gagged and turned her face, squeezing shut her eyes. Warrick wrapped his arm around her, tucked her head under his chin.

"Renil." The name fell from her mouth like another glop.

"Did he kill you? Or did he wrong you in another way?"

She wrapped swollen fingers around her throat. "Throw."

"From the bridge?" It was almost always so when the ghosts were near to one. At her nod, he asked, "What village?"

She pointed north.

"I will find him. Do you mark your body?"

She pointed to the mud at her feet.

"I will have your people come for you. What name will they know you by?"

Her blackened tongue pushed more mud from her mouth. "Fajana."

"Have you another wrong to right—whether against you or committed by you?"

She shook her head.

"I will right this one, as soon as can be done. Good journey to the end, Fajana."

He reined Troll back toward Iarthil, who waited at the foot of the bridge, with the knights peering uneasily around them. "I will continue on to the next village, where I must right a wrong. Let us take Elina back to the carriage. When I am done, I will catch up to you."

"Right a wrong?" Iarthil glanced to the river. "Why? How?"

"Serjeant," Elina said, lifting her head, revealing a face nearly as pale as the ghost's hair. "Whatever Warrick is saying that he must do for that poor woman, let him do it. We will ask our questions later."

Though he clearly wished to ask them now, the serjeant nodded. "Of course, Your Highness."

She exhaled a shaky breath, then touched her fingertips to the glowing lines on his bicep. "I know not whether to call this a curse or a gift."

Warrick hadn't known either. Not for a long time.

But it was a gift.

Night fell before Warrick reached the camp. At the prison, the serjeant had warned him to stay away until dawn if he arrived after the rising of the evening star. Warrick would not. He had just begun to debate how best to penetrate the camp's defenses when Iarthil himself rode out to meet him.

"What happened?"

Warrick had ridden to the village, found Renil, and hauled him into the market square. There he'd announced what Renil had done—and when the man refused to confess, Warrick had tied him behind Troll and dragged him to the bridge, with most of the villagers following. By touching Warrick, they'd all been able to see for themselves whom Renil had wronged.

Though it was not true of every murderer he'd found, Warrick hadn't needed to kill Renil himself. Instead the villagers had seen justice done—and Fajana had gone.

Never would he regret doing what was right. But his gut had twisted into knots upon the realization that, in his absence, Elina had likely drunk a tonic prepared by Chardryn. The dose of bloodbane would not harm her worse than it already had—but it meant the purge would end a day later than it would have.

And Warrick was in no mood to answer Iarthil's demand. "Elina will ask me soon enough. Let me only tell it once."

The other man nodded. "Do all the dead become ghosts?"

"The dead who were wronged—and only if they stay until it is made right. And the dead who committed a wrong, until it is made right."

"Those who were wronged. Murdered?"

"Often."

"Then you could speak to Elina's mother—or *I* could, as long as I touched you."

Warrick grunted a confirmation.

Iarthil stared straight ahead. "If the opportunity comes, I would ask it of you. There is a wrong *I* have done that I would wish undone."

Such as promising not to lead Elina home? But Warrick held his tongue. He could hardly comprehend the sort of honor that placed a vow made to a dead woman above the harm done to the living.

"If the opportunity comes," he said.

Warrick was accustomed to the endless questions that followed the discovery that he could see ghosts, along with the requests to speak to every dead relation that someone ever had. So he was prepared to sit at the fire and give answers. It was made all the more tedious by the need to wait for Iarthil to repeat every question and answer in the proper language—but with Elina at his side, easily bearable.

Until she raised an eyebrow just so, and teased that—after the curse took her—she would make him into a living lantern by following him.

Then he could bear it no longer. Iarthil had not even finished his translation before Warrick hauled her up into his arms and strode to her tent. From behind him came the flapping and fluttering of the attendants.

Warrick roared over his shoulder, "Tell them I will strip her myself before bathing her with my tongue!"

Elina was still giggling uncontrollably when he laid her on the bed. Then his body came down over hers and her laughter quieted, melting into a soft sigh against his mouth.

"It is a gift," she murmured decisively. "Just as you have been to me."

Again he was upended. But this time, Warrick understood it. Anyone from the Dead Lands would have understood *this*, the most basic of all lessons. For what was magic but an unseen power that changed the world? And of all true magics, love was the most powerful—so loving Elina had overturned his entire world.

Just as he intended to overturn hers.

He captured her mouth, and the faint bitterness struck at his heart. Lifting his head, hoarsely he told her, "Not until you are well again will I leave your side. This I swear to you, Elina."

She bit her lip, eyes searching his. "What did you just promise?"

"To always love you." He clasped her hand and brought it to his chest. "My heart is yours. My axe is yours. My last breath is yours."

Wonderingly she touched his face. "I know not what you say. But this is how I always dreamed someone might one day look at me. As if I were loved."

"You *are* loved, woman." Warrick lowered his head. "I will show you how much."

With his mouth. With his tongue. With his hands. Until she screamed for him as she came, then whispered that she was dead. And he loved her even more when she pushed his head back down between her thighs and asked him to kill her again.

WARRICK awoke.

Something was wrong.

Not Elina sleeping in his arms. Not the moonlight faintly illuminating the tent. But the dull gleam of a blade, a shadow moving past the curtains—

Warrick whipped around, grabbed his axe and hurled it at the shadow. The loud clatter of chain ended with a solid *thunk*.

Elina bolted up to sitting. "Warrick?"

"Shh. All is well." Except for the bed curtains. The stains might never come out. He drew her into his arms and leaned back against the pillows. "I merely righted another wrong."

She hummed against his throat. Already drifting into sleep again, her body soft and warm against his.

He closed his eyes and joined her.

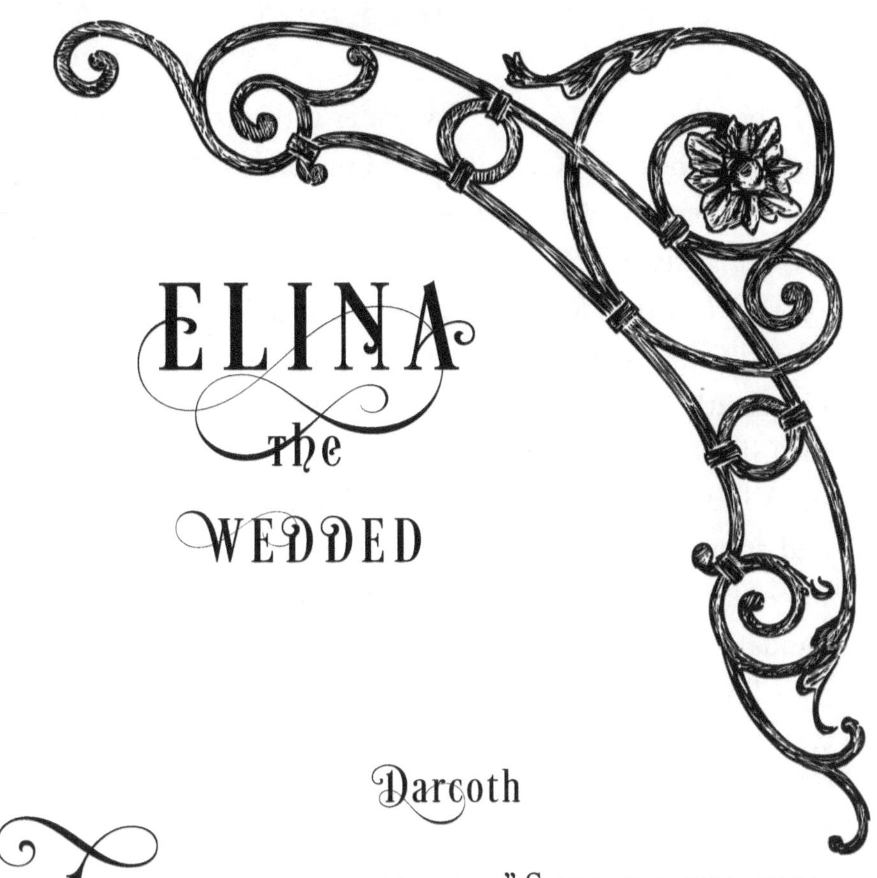

ELINA the WEDDED

Darçoth

"I HARDLY KNOW WHAT TO SAY." STILL FLUSHED FROM the *very* thorough morning kiss that Warrick had just given to her, Elina stared at the assassin lying on the floor of her tent with Warrick's axe embedded in his skull. "If I were Nanny Char, I might mutter that barbarians never pick up their mess. Or perhaps I should say how glad I am that my attendants no longer come in until I call for them. But all I can think is that I was not the only one you killed last night."

Warrick merely cocked an arm behind his head and looked arrogantly pleased with himself.

"Is there a ghost in here now?" But a glance at his chest

told her that there wasn't. "I wonder if this is one of the bizarre things that Chardryn told me of. You kissed me quite ardently—*everywhere*—while knowing a corpse was lying there."

When he only looked even more smug, she snorted out a laugh. Then she crawled back onto the bed and kissed his mouth. "I thank you for protecting me, Warrick of the Ghost Clan."

All humor fled his expression. He clasped her nape and spoke roughly, fiercely. The same way he'd spoken to her last night. The same way he'd used his mouth and hands and tongue.

Elina had begun to love it when he spoke to her that way. Even better would be understanding what he said. "Today I'm going to teach you two words in my language. Kiss," she said—and demonstrated. "Kiss."

Warrick grinned. "Kiss."

She rewarded him with one. "I'll decide on the other word later. But now I'd better let Serjeant Iarthil know that an assassin slipped through his defenses."

WHILE RIDING WITH WARRICK THAT day, she taught him 'axe.' The next morning was 'tongue.' Then 'horse.' By the time they neared Darcoth on Midsummer's Eve, Elina could almost speak to him a full sentence about kissing his horse with her tongue while eating a raspberry in bed, and Serjeant Iarthil had almost stopped apologizing for his "blasted selfish decision to keep our perimeter open after dark, simply so that I could satisfy our curiosity about what happened with the ghost and the village."

But it was while the serjeant was riding beside them, apologizing again, that Warrick said something that stopped him short. Which they then discussed back and forth without any translation until Elina was forced to break in with a sharp, "Serjeant?"

He looked at her, abashed. "He says the issue is not the perimeter, but how they managed to find you."

They'd *always* managed to find her. "I assume my uncle lays out gold enough for the assassins to bribe people to talk."

"The barbarian thinks it is more likely the gold crown and paint. It causes a stir and makes it easier for an assassin to follow our route."

Which was something Serjeant Iarthil had said before, when they'd first fled Aleron and Tagdon. He'd argued that they ought to appear as wealthy merchants. Or lesser nobles, at best. Yet he'd been countered by Lady Faraine, who'd pointed out that they sought allies and protection, and most royal courts would never acknowledge mere merchants or lesser nobles. When the Radiant Queen arrived in their realm, however, they were eager to welcome her.

Though she despised saying it, Elina told him, "Lady Faraine wasn't wrong."

"She wasn't," he admitted. "Yet our circumstances are different now—you have already made allies in the realms we will be traveling through. And it is likely no coincidence that this assassin so quickly found you after you wore the queen's face in Torrath. It had been quite some time since the last one found us…and it had been quite some time since you wore the paint."

"But we marry tomorrow." Though she would give near anything not to be trembling under the weight of the royal raiments as she spoke her vows, Elina could not simply discard tradition.

"Wear a gold dress, then—it will not be out of place amid the Midsummer festivities. Wear the crown inside Khides' temple, if you must. But forego the queen's face." The corner of his mouth twitched. "Do not forget he said you are more lovely without it."

Never would she forget that. She leaned back against Warrick's chest, suddenly bubbling with happiness. "We marry tomorrow!"

Smiling, Serjeant Iarthil translated her happy statement to Warrick. He bent his head to her ear, and rumbled an equally short reply in a voice that sent shivers racing over her skin and arousal heating everything within.

"What does it mean?" she asked the serjeant, then repeated Warrick's reply as closely as she could.

Warrick began laughing behind her as Serjeant Iarthil turned quite red. "It means 'We can'"—he mumbled something she didn't catch—"'tomorrow.'"

"We can what?"

And that was how Elina learned the barbarian word 'fuck.'

. . .

On Midsummer morn, barely a moment passed between Elina calling for her attendants and Chardryn charging into the tent with a battalion of maids armed with buckets of steaming water, lotions, and brushes. The nurse shooed a naked Warrick off to his breakfast, tossed his wrap and boots out after him, then seized Elina—who was bathed and buffed and plucked until there was not a single hair remaining below her neck and not a single curl astray above it. Then she was wrapped in gold silk, perfumed, and polished—and finally declared ready to wed by the old nurse, who promptly burst into tears.

But this was a day for laughing, not for crying. Elina soon teased Chardryn out of her tears, and was sent off to marry with her Nanny Char scowling in the way Elina had loved for so long.

Armor shining and hair trimmed, Serjeant Iarthil met her outside the tent. "You are truly radiant, my queen."

She *felt* radiant. "I thank you, Serjeant. You are also looking very well. Your beard is charmingly tamed."

"Nanny accosted me when my defenses were down."

"She was on a rampage," Elina agreed. "I wonder if she intends to oil my husband-to-be? I've noted her appreciation for the way his muscles gleam."

Though if Nanny Char had caught him, he'd already washed it away. Dripping from his bath, Warrick strode across the camp, leading his horse and wearing only his axe on his back.

Elina could not take her eyes from him. "Do you suppose that is the traditional wedding attire in the Dead Lands?"

"I hardly know, Your Highness."

"Perhaps he is merely eager. And efficient. Ask him if he intends to consummate our marriage before we even leave the temple."

"I beg you to teach him more words, my queen, so that you might ask him yourself."

"I might call to him with the word you taught me yesterday. If I say it enough, perhaps he will not even wait until we reach the altar."

Looking pained, the serjeant spoke in the eastern tongue.

Warrick grinned at Elina, causing her heart to skip. Then he dropped his horse's reins, apparently leaving the beast to stomp about the camp like a drunken mammoth, and vanished into the attendants' tent.

Elina eyed her man-at-arms curiously. "Did you truly ask him what I told you to? I expected some reply."

"I told him that you were admiring the swing of his mighty weapon and that you would like to see it oiled."

She gave a delighted laugh. "Well done, Serjeant!"

A faint smile curved his mouth. After a moment, he asked quietly, "You will be happy?"

"I am already," she said. The serjeant nodded, then blinked and looked away, but not before she saw the glint in his eyes.

At this rate, Elina would be the only one who did *not* cry today.

Though perhaps Warrick would join her in laughing. He emerged from the tent carrying her tonic in one hand and a length of gold silk in the other. The cup he gave to her; the silk he knotted around his waist.

Apparently Nanny Char's rampage had continued. At least his wrap was still efficient. He only needed to lift it.

Anticipation thrummed through her. "Ready, then?"

Warrick's dark eyes met hers. Without a word, he plucked the cup from her fingers and tossed it over his shoulder in the general direction of the tent. Elina was the next to be tossed, though he made certain she landed astride his horse. He swung up into the saddle behind her.

"Onward," she said—and they were off to be wed.

MIDSUMMER BEING THE LONGEST DAY of the year, when they entered the city many revelers were already in the streets, celebrating the full length of the day. Elina tossed to them the gold coins that Serjeant Iarthil and his knights had brought along for the purpose of sharing the Radiant Queen's joy.

She had plenty of joy to share.

Marble columns ringed the outside of Khides' temple. The entrance was flanked by two stone statues, both ancient warrior-kings with the heads of wolves. The sun was high overhead, the shadows short.

Midday on Midsummer—there could not be a finer

time for the Radiant Queen to wed.

As soon as they dismounted, Elina clasped Warrick's hand and pulled him up the steps, abandoning the heat outside for the coolness within. The serjeant's and the knights' boots clapped rhythmically behind her. Ahead stood the priestess, garbed in a simple black robe.

"Welcome," said she in the southern tongue, then glanced at Warrick. She spoke what Elina assumed was the same greeting, but in the eastern tongue. Her gaze continued on to the knights. "You are here to wed or to invade?"

Elina grinned and bounced up onto her toes. "Wed."

"So you shall. You have a red ribbon?"

"I have it here, my lady." Serjeant Iarthil produced the crimson length.

"Then give to me your hands." The priestess repeated the instruction to Warrick. Elina's heart thumped wildly as he threaded his fingers through hers, his dark eyes locked on her face.

"Your names?"

"Elina of Aleron."

"*The Radiant Queen* of Aleron," the serjeant emphasized.

The priestess's gaze flicked to his face and narrowed, but she said nothing. Only looked then to Warrick. Her brows rose when he spoke his reply. Yet again, she said nothing, and began winding the ribbon around their clasped hands.

"Elina and Warrick are not yet bound together. So

we gather to witness their joining, as two…be-become…one." Her voice faltered as her fingers brushed over Elina's rings. She drew her hands back. "You ought not wear such jewels when you speak your vows."

Face hardening, Warrick spoke harshly to her in response.

"He says that you cannot take them off," Serjeant Iarthil murmured to Elina. "That they keep you alive."

The priestess glanced to Elina's face, as if searching for the reason why.

Sick dread boiled in her chest. "A curse," Elina told her. "A wasting disease. Why must I not wear them?"

"The power the jewels hold—you cannot know what such magic will make of the vows you speak, what spell it might cast…and what it might do if you choose to unbind." She looked to Warrick and repeated her explanation.

His brows snapped together upon the last word.

"He asks what it means to unbind. The priestess says that it means to unmarry."

Warrick scoffed.

"He says there is no such thing."

"There is," Elina said and let the serjeant translate her reply as she spoke it. "Not in Aleron, but in other realms through which we've traveled. If a couple marries, and one of them unknots the ribbon, the marriage is undone as if the wedding never occurred. If one of them cuts the ribbon, each take from their home the possessions that are theirs alone, and thereafter they are as if dead to each other."

"Here in Darcoth, that is the way," said the priestess.

Warrick clasped her hand tighter, his gaze boring into hers. His words were sharp, fierce—but with a hint of uncertainty that pierced through her heart.

"He asks if you intend to one day unmarry him. He asks if such a spell would matter at all."

"Even if I had long to live, it would not matter. I would never wish to unmarry," she said, her throat suddenly clogged with her roiling emotions. Some sweet. Some painful. But she would not cry this day. She turned to the priestess. "Let us speak our vows."

"You are certain?"

Elina nodded. As did Warrick, when Khides' priestess repeated the question.

"Very well, then." She again took up the ribbon, threading it through their entangled fingers and around their wrists. "Elina of Aleron, do you pledge yourself to this man and vow to be his faithful wife?"

Happiness began to rise again through the dread and fear that had been weighing heavily in her stomach. "I will."

"Warrick of the Ghost Clan"—she paused and switched languages to finish the vow.

Warrick's gaze burned into Elina's as he replied.

The priestess knotted the ribbon. "Then you are now wife and husband."

With a relieved laugh, Warrick dragged Elina forward by their bound hands and kissed her, so thoroughly that he might as well have consummated their marriage right there.

"The ribbon must bind your hands until dawn," the priestess reminded them when Warrick finally released Elina. "I suggest you take close care of it after."

In Aleron, the ribbon could be tossed away after dawn—though some brides kept theirs for the memory of it. But Elina would happily follow the priestess's suggestion. This was a memory she would always keep near.

"My queen." Serjeant Iarthil bowed to Elina. Then to Warrick. "My king."

Behind him, the knights went down to one knee.

Warrick laughed and shook his head at their display, then scooped Elina into his arms. He strode for the temple's exit.

"Keep up, Serjeant!" Elina called back to him, laughing. "We have songs to sing and wine to drink and a feast to eat! And you, my king—" She looked up at Warrick and twined her arms around his neck. "You need to take me to bed."

Though Elina wished to, they could not go directly to her tent. The songs and the wine and the feasts celebrated Midsummer Day, but also celebrated her marriage and welcomed her king consort. She could not deny her people the opportunity to do both—especially as there were so few here to celebrate with.

Had she the energy, she might have danced. Had she

not feared puking, she would have feasted. But she could sing and sip a little wine, and so she did until her voice was raw and her limbs were loose and warm. With her hand bound to Warrick's, she could not leave his side—nor did she wish to. Quite frequently, he would kiss the breath from her, and she spent nearly the entire afternoon sitting on his lap and nestled back against his chest.

It was nearing sunset when he abruptly lifted her into his arms and carried her toward the tent, accompanied by the cheers and whistles of her entire retinue.

And so it was time.

Arousal flowed through her veins like warmed honey, sweet and thick. Each of his kisses struck her anew. It was her *husband* kissing her now. It was her husband setting Elina on her feet with his free hand searching her hair for pins, so that her curls tumbled down her back. It was her husband sliding the gold silk from her shoulders and pressing kisses to her throat.

And it was her king who braced his forearm under her bottom, lifting her and carrying her to the bed. Her king who followed her down, groaning when she opened her thighs so that he could settle into the warmest, wettest part of her.

How could his mouth please her so much more now that they had wed? Was it the vow they'd spoken?— because each kiss and lick seemed to bring her near to the edge of dying.

And he *devoured* her. With their bound hands clasped

on her belly, her knees hooked over his shoulders. His mouth made her body writhe and her hips roll, as if all of the energy she'd saved not dancing at the celebration had been reserved so that she might dance to the rhythm of his tongue over *that* spot, whirling her tighter and tighter—until he lifted his head and she felt unfamiliar pressure at her entrance. Her approaching orgasm fled. Warrick grunted softly against her flesh before huffing a short laugh. But before she could wonder what amused him, his hand between her legs shifted position and a finger was sliding within, pressing and rubbing. Then his tongue found that spot again.

Oh gods. She gripped the sheet, then his head, then her breast. Warrick was *inside* her—and licking her, and she could only writhe, and cry his name, and grip his beribboned hand, and live and live and live. The honey in her blood seemed to surge downward to drench his finger and his tongue, and the roll of her hips became a tense coiling within. Then the coil snapped, and she screamed from between clenched teeth, her inner muscles clamping down upon his finger as if to keep him locked inside.

Yet she could not. Withdrawing his hand, Warrick murmured her name and kissed her belly. Her legs slid bonelessly from his shoulders as he rose up between her thighs, his fist gripping his long jutting shaft. He slicked the broad crown of it through her honeyed wetness, riding the thick length up over that too-sensitive bit of flesh. Elina gasped his name, and tilted her hips toward him, and he did it again.

"Elina." He spoke more words, his voice deep. Guttural. He sucked in a breath between his clenched teeth and thrust upward again, tunneling through her swollen folds.

But not inside her.

Elina squirmed, and twisted, and tried to make him go where she wanted, where she was aching and hollow. Yet he only braced his elbow beside her shoulder and leaned into each drive of his hips, the hot column of flesh relentlessly slipping and sliding over the bud that he'd licked.

"Warrick!" She sobbed his name, her thighs clasping tight to his sides. His hand gripped her ass and angled her up higher, fingers digging into her soft flesh, a rasping groan tearing from his throat with every hard thrust. His head dropped, his mouth near her ear as he growled her name, then growled something more, fierce and rough and demanding. And the coil within burst again, in endless waves that must have caught Warrick in their wake, for he snapped his hips forward hard, and again. He groaned deep and pumped his pulsing shaft through her sodden cleft, his big body tense and shaking.

Then he slowed, kissing her, deep and wet before throwing his head back to heave giant breaths—still rocking between her legs, though his flesh was softening now and his seed was smeared over her belly.

Just as he'd done the previous nights. Yet she had not expected the same on her wedding night.

Elina slid her foot up the back of his thigh, trying to puzzle through it. She *was* utterly satisfied and yet…well, truthfully, she'd thought to feel more than his finger inside her. "I cannot decide whether you've been attempting a bizarre method of putting a baby in through my navel, or if there was a ghost squashed between us and you were fucking her instead."

Warrick choked. Then he burst out with a great laugh, his head hanging, his shoulders shaking.

Her own laugh joined his, utterly surprised and delighted that she'd made him…that she'd made him…

Her laughter died. Her heart shriveled.

"No, Elina. Do not—!" Urgently Warrick caught her when she tried to roll out from beneath him, tried to rip her hand from the ribbon. His eyes were dark, his expression anguished as his fingers tightened around hers, locking their palms together, stopping her from escaping the ribbon's bond. "Do not unmarry me, Elina, I beg you. Listen to me. *Listen.* I intended to speak with you this night. You—"

"Liar!"

Her eyes and throat burned with unshed tears. But she was not going to cry on this day. She was not.

Not over him.

"I spoke no lies." He pinned her body with the massive strength of his. "I sought the truth."

"The truth of what? Never have *I* lied to—"

"Not you. *About* you. And the curse. Elina—"

"What truth do you wish to know? That I puke until I spit blood? That every joint in my body aches even while I'm lying in bed? That—"

"*You aren't cursed.*" He hissed fiercely through his teeth. "You aren't cursed, Elina! You've been poisoned."

She stilled. Wildly her gaze searched his face. He met her eyes unwaveringly, his expression hard and intense. As if he wanted nothing more than to make her believe him. But how could she believe? How?

"Elina." His voice gentled. "My wife. My heart is yours. My life is yours. My axe is yours. Do not fight me now. Let me fight for you."

Her body was shaking. "Who?"

"Chardryn."

"No." Elina shook her head, the tears she'd fought spurting from her eyes. "No."

"Mayhap I'm wrong." But his expression said that he didn't believe it.

"Tell me." The command scraped from her raw throat.

"The doxweed is not—"

"No." The curse, her poisoning, it was *nothing*. She'd known not to trust anyone. But she'd trusted *him*. "Why did you pretend not to understand?"

He sighed heavily. "That was nothing to do with you. It began in the prison—delaying the search for the people we'd freed."

"We?"

"Bannin. A friend. He made certain they sailed, then

killed Lord Gleris."

"Good," she whispered.

He grunted his agreement. "When you came to my cell, the warden already believed I could not understand him. It would have been foolish to reveal that I could then."

"Yes. But after?"

"As soon as we met again, you were taken by the mud-beast—and when I breathed into your mouth, I tasted the bloodbane."

"Bloodbane?"

"The poison. So I continued the pretense to discover who had done it, and why you were made to believe it a curse. People speak unguardedly when they believe you do not understand."

"As I did," she said bitterly. "I *was* a fool to trust you."

His face whitened into a bleak mask. A muscle in his jaw flexed, as if he intended to speak and only ended up clenching his teeth. Silently he stared down at her, his throat working as he swallowed, and swallowed, and swallowed again.

She had done the same before, when trying to dislodge a painful lump of emotion in her throat. Now, witnessing his struggle, she had one, too. And a horrible ache in her chest where her heart had been, seeing how her words had sliced him so deeply.

Why was *his* pain hurting *her*?

"I have wronged you." The words came out so thick and guttural, it was as if Warrick had swallowed them, too.

He raised shaking fingers to her face, but did not touch her before clenching his hand and drawing it away. "I only meant to discover who was poisoning you, and then to save you. I had not intended to hurt you—but that is what I did. So I will make it right."

Make it right. That, she believed he would do. From all that Elina knew of him, of the ghost he'd seen and his actions then, he *would* make right a wrong.

She closed her eyes. Breathed deep. Tried to look past the emotions crushing her chest. He truly did have good reason for the deception in the prison. And after realizing she was being poisoned, he'd had good reason to continue the pretense.

"I just…I wish that you had told *me* that you understood." She sighed. "But then I would have made you tell me *why* you were pretending."

"I knew not what you would do. I knew not if you would trust me, or if you would speak of the poison to someone and place yourself in danger if they feared discovery."

And give Elina a huge dose of bloodbane to finish her off. "Is it the tonic?"

"Yes."

So he'd begun to make it himself. "Do you truly have a custom of caring for a bride for three days?"

"Not custom, but it *is* my preference."

"Ah!" A shaky laugh escaped her. "You *did* lie!"

"So I did. I am not sorry for it."

"You should not be. You harmed no one…and helped

me." She bit her lip, studying his face. His eyes seemed darker than ever, but a small hope had begun to bleed through the bleakness that had overtaken his countenance when she'd declared she was a fool for trusting him. But was she? "Why did you marry me?"

"To protect you. To help you return to Aleron and kill your uncle." His voice roughened as his throat worked again. "And because I love you. You've overturned my world, Elina. The moment I first saw your face."

She pressed a hand over her eyes but still they overfilled in a deluge of overwhelming emotion. "And you would not just say that without meaning it?" she sobbed quietly. "Because of what I confessed to you that night?"

How pitifully desperate she was to be loved.

"Never, Elina." He lowered his brow to hers. "Never. I loved you already that night. Your strength. Your kindness. Your teasing. You cannot know how many times I nearly revealed myself by laughing."

At that Elina could only cry more, for she had wanted him to laugh with her on this day. Yet now she was sobbing, unable to stop. Warrick had given to her everything she desperately wanted, had spoken aloud the words she'd yearned to hear for so long. He'd given his heart to her, and now Elina was afraid to trust that it was true. Though she wanted to so badly. To grab hold of the love he offered, and to believe in it, and hold it close to her own heart. To hold *him* close.

Did she dare?

Elina knew not if she could. And whatever choice she made, she must stop crying first.

She *must*.

Slowly she quieted and dragged in a shuddering breath. "And then you *did* laugh."

With her. Fulfilling one of her wedding day wishes. And as painful as the truth revealed by that laughter had proven to be, was she not glad to know? Was she not glad now to speak with him unhindered?

She was. She truly was.

"I had just completed a magnificent spend over my comely wife, one that near ripped my soul from my flesh along with my seed, and you asked if I was fucking a ghost. I could no more have stopped that laugh than I could have stopped the sun rising." Warrick gave to her a wry smile. "Though I truly meant to speak with you this night—I had hoped that during these three days alone we could decide how to act. Though at the same time, I wished never to tell you. I never wanted to see you hurt."

"Hurt because of what you did or what you think Chardryn did?"

"Chardryn. Never did I consider that you would see what *I* did as a hurtful deception. My only thought was of you, Elina. So I assumed that was all you would see, too. I *am* sorry for that. Though I know not what else I might have done, what better choice there was, never did I want to hurt you. That is opposite of what I meant to do." He paused. "I *am* a thickheaded brute."

Caught by surprise, Elina sputtered out an amused, "You truly are!"

"And I *will* fuck you in bizarre ways. Like a pig."

She laughed aloud. "Oh, gods. You heard that, too? Oh! Oh! And you will drag me from the tent when you get stuck in me!" With her fingers she wiped her eyes. "But what of this night? Despite what Nanny Char says, I *will* survive your massive size."

Nanny Char. Her mirth instantly vanished. So did his.

"Two reasons," he said. "The first is that I can only get my littlest finger into you."

She frowned at him, bewildered. Then realization struck. "I can remove the rings."

"Not even for a moment." Expression harsh, he shook his head. His beribboned fingers tightened on hers. "Until you purge the poison from your body, not for a moment will you remove the jewels. Not a single moment. Swear it to me."

"I swear it," she whispered, struck by his urgency. Struck by his concern. "What is the second reason?"

"Never have I lain with anyone but you. Once I am inside your cunt, I might burst after one thrust. And if you get with child before your body is purged—"

Oh. "The poison might harm a growing baby."

"A growing baby might harm *you*. The purge will be worse than your disease."

A tremor of dread shook through her. "And after?"

"You will be better. Mayhap not as well as before the

poison. But not ill."

Then it would be worth the pain. "And you believe it is Nurse Chardryn who did it?"

"I do."

Elina pulled a shaky breath. "Tell me why."

WARRICK
the
BEDDED

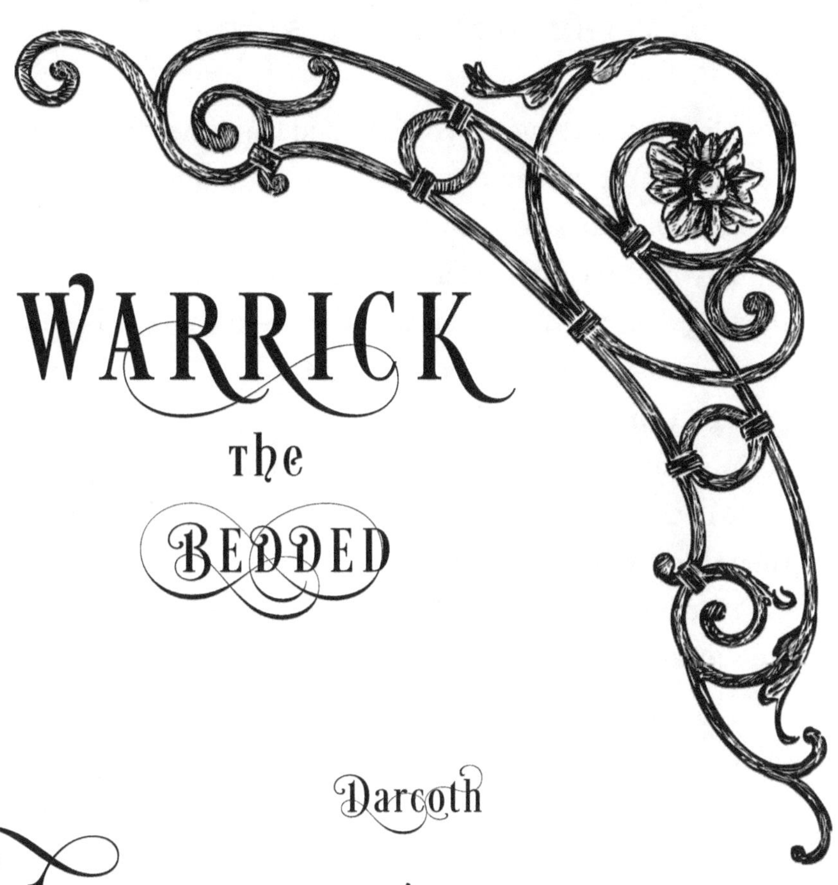

Darcoth

IN THE SAME MANNER SHE'D LAIN WITH HIM BEFORE—face to face on the pillow as she told him of her betrayals—they did again now as Warrick told her of the poison. Aware of how his voice might carry through the tent walls despite the ongoing music and celebration, quietly Warrick explained what he'd learned in these past days of helping Chardryn prepare the tonic. How he'd attempted to determine whether anyone else could have altered the contents in the apothecary chest without her knowledge—for five years ongoing—and how her familiarity with each herb and powder was contradictory to her simple mistake with the doxweed.

Elina listened intently, their bound hands nestled under her cheek. Yet when her question came, it was not about Chardryn. "How do *you* know it is a simple mistake?"

"My mother is a healer. A witch. We were to become the same—me, my brothers and sister—and so she began teaching us as soon as we could speak."

"Yet you left the Dead Lands and your clan?" Her curious gaze searched his. "Because you could see ghosts?"

"My curse or my gift," he said. "I knew not what it was then. I left to discover that answer."

"And helped people. Not only the dead, but those alive who loved them."

"I have tried. Wrongs cannot truly be righted. The dead cannot be given life again."

"Yet it is *something* to offer them justice. You could have turned your head and pretended not to see." With her free hand, she reached out to caress his jaw. "It is bravely done."

His chest ached with the sweetness of that light touch—the first time she had deliberately reached out to him since discovering his deception. She had not fully forgiven him. Likely did not fully trust him.

More probably, she'd merely decided to trust him *more* than everyone else who had deceived her…and whom she now trusted not at all.

She withdrew her hand with a heavy sigh. "We must decide what to do next. We must continue onward, of course. Yet Chardryn's betrayal will be deeply felt by all."

"We will go west."

"West? But—" Her brows drew together. Sudden wariness shuttered her gaze. "Is it *not* dangerous?"

"No more than anywhere else," he said softly, knowing the painful conclusion she'd already drawn. "I have friends in Galoth who can assist us. It will be the fastest route for you to return home."

Flatly she said, "Serjeant Iarthil is keeping me from Aleron."

"It would seem. He has said that he regrets a vow he made but—"

"He will not rescind it." It was not a question. She likely knew Iarthil too well to believe he would.

"Not until he speaks to your mother."

She huffed a short, disbelieving laugh and rolled onto her back, staring up at the roof of the tent. In a dull voice, she said, "It seems I have no tears left. Or no expectations of loyalty from anyone, so I feel no pain or surprise."

Or she'd suffered so many blows, numbness had set in. Heart aching for her, he gently clasped tighter their beribboned fingers. "I keep in my mind the names of those who have betrayed you, wife. My axe's journey need not begin and end with your uncle Soren. Simply speak it into truth."

A more genuine laugh broke from her—and with it, he thought, some of the numbness cracked, for she pressed her forearm across her eyes. "I did not want to believe it of Serjeant Iarthil," she said in a voice thick with tears.

"Though I knew. These past two years—after the jewels landed in my lap—I have been pushing harder for us to return. After all, the rings could protect me from my uncle. A part of me assumed that was what I was *meant* to do. For why would a raven drop them into my lap if not to help free my people? But Serjeant Iarthil insisted we continue searching for the warrior from the prophecy, claiming that the jewels alone would not protect me from Soren. We needed the axe, too." She gave a bitter little laugh. "Now I will return to Aleron with both the axe *and* the jewels, and if I survive the purge, I might even live long enough to see my uncle felled—but I wonder what sort of queen I am that everyone is so ready to betray me."

A sharp claw seemed stuck in his heart. "You will not have the jewels when we reach Aleron."

She lifted her arm from her eyes and frowned at him. "What do you mean?"

"They are the Stars of Anhera. You know of the stone sickness in Galoth?"

A single nod was her answer, her gaze intent on his.

He rubbed the tips of his entwined fingers across her rings. "These were stolen from the goddess ten years past. When they are returned, it will break the curse."

"Break the—" Horror widened her eyes. "I have had them for two *years*, Warrick. Two years! How many suffered who did not have to?"

Emotion swelled in his throat. He brought their clasped hands to his lips and kissed her fingers. "*That* is the sort of queen you are. You would have died when you gave back the jewels. Yet your first thought is this—for people who are not even of your kingdom."

"I have been resigned to dying. Relieving such suffering would be a fine way to go." Despite her light reply, another frown furrowed her brow. "A raven is Anhera's bird."

"And the jewels kept you alive long enough to come to my prison…then put you on a path to Galoth, and to regain your health before arriving with the jewels to break the curse. Then on to Aleron, with my axe. So mayhaps it *was* meant to be that you received the jewels and went home. Only not as you thought."

"Not as I ever thought." She rolled to face him again. Softly she said, "I cannot remain with my retinue. They cannot *all* be disloyal, but I would always be on my guard with them. The people who feed me, who bathe me…not knowing if some helped either Nurse Chardryn or Serjeant Iarthil." She shook her head. "I have too little trust left."

"I will take you to Galoth. Only you and me."

Though her expression brightened, she hesitated. "What of when the purge comes? Will you need assistance?"

As if he would allow anyone else to see to his wife's needs. "We will take the river route. I can tend to you on the barge."

"Is there anyone in this retinue I can trust fully? What have your overhearings told you?"

Warrick considered that. "The maid, Dara," he said after a moment. "You wish her to come with us?"

Elina shook her head. "There needs to be someone we can trust to stand as witness and speak to the true reasons I left." A brittle smile curved her lips. "The serjeant's vow to keep me safe means he would not obey any order to lead the retinue home and to let us continue alone. You would have to kill him to stop him from accompanying us."

"If you wish, I will."

"No. But I wish never to see him again." With that fierce statement, more of her hurt slipped through another crack in her numbness.

He cupped her cheek. "They do not expect us to leave this tent for three days. We can be gone before they are aware."

"Yet if we sneak away, they will not know why." A hint of vulnerability glimmered in her eyes. "And…I wish to know why Nanny Char betrayed me. Perhaps it ought not matter, but it does."

"Then we will ask her. We can call for her now, claiming that my bizarre and giant cock is stuck inside you and we need her assistance, lest I pull you ass to ass from the tent."

Elina grinned and bit her lip, as if against a laugh. Then her expression softened. "How long will the purge last?"

"A fortnight for the worst of it. Then recovering your strength after…it will take longer."

"And in that time we will not wish to kiss much. Or do more."

"I think not." Kissing was the very last thing Warrick would wish to do when she was suffering.

"When will the purge begin?"

She had not taken the bloodbane since the day of his last glowing. "Within the next day or two."

"Let us be gone before then." She drew a shuddering breath. "But *this* night… I would wish to have something to hold onto—and to look forward to when the purge is over. So let us not be quiet anymore. Let them hear me cry your name as you eat me alive. Let them quake at the sound of your mighty roar as you spend, and let all the world know the Radiant Queen has thoroughly bedded—and been bedded by—her king."

Swiftly she moved, pushing at Warrick's shoulder until he rolled onto his back. A moment later she straddled his stomach, and he was torn between arousal and laughter and the deep ache of knowing that Elina was not merely building a memory to carry her through the purge, but trying to forget how painfully she'd been betrayed by those closest to her.

Yet if forgetting was what she needed, then he would drive every coherent thought from her brain. Clasping her nape, he dragged her mouth to his. Almost near enough to kiss. "You wish to be eaten alive, wife?" he growled. "You wish me to feast upon your cunt?"

Her skin flushed. "Yes," she said breathlessly.

"Then you are astride the wrong part of me." As her eyes widened, he began to urge her higher, his mouth already watering. He reverently kissed the flesh that passed over his lips, from her chin to her belly, until her bare cunt hovered over his mouth—wet and luscious and fragrant. Had any man ever been so blessed? Warrick marveled at the exquisite beauty of her—his woman, his wife, his queen—then lifted his head to partake in the finest of all wedding feasts.

This one began with the sweets.

WARRICK SLIPPED INTO THE ATTENDANTS' tent shortly after dawn. In the pale light, he quickly located Dara's bed and cupped a palm over the maid's mouth.

Her eyes flew open. He gestured for her silence.

When she nodded, he removed his hand from her mouth. Worry pinched her expression—fearing what had brought him to seek her out.

The queen? she mouthed.

"Wake Chardryn," he murmured. "Come to the royal tent. Have her bring her apothecary chest. Quietly."

Again she nodded—then eyed him strangely. Likely because he'd spoken the northern tongue, as everyone from Aleron did.

"Quickly," he said.

She scrambled from bed and was shaking Chardryn awake when Warrick left the tent.

He returned to Elina's still-darkened tent, found her already dressed in her riding trousers and a plain tunic. Her small bundle of clothing and gold purse, he'd already added to Troll's saddlebags. They would leave immediately after confronting Chardryn, while most of the camp was still sleeping off a night of revelry.

Glancing about the tent, he searched for the red ribbon that had bound their hands until dawn. His heart swelled when he spotted it. Elina had looped the ribbon around her wrist until it formed a bracelet.

Swiftly he kissed her, lifted her hand to kiss her palm and the ribbon that had married them, then strapped on his axe.

When Dara and Chardryn arrived, Elina was sitting at her table, lighting a small lantern. Breakfast was arrayed before her. She poured water into a goblet from a carafe.

If the nurse suffered from lack of sleep, it was not apparent by Chardryn's sharp gaze. "Are you well, my queen?"

Warrick's chest tightened, for the lantern revealed Elina was clearly not—her face pale and her expression tight. Though whether the strain she felt was due to the little sleep they'd enjoyed, the oncoming purge, or the emotional toll of what was about to occur, he didn't know.

"Sit with me. You as well, Dara." She poured a goblet of water for each. Gingerly the maid sat on Elina's left. Chardryn placed her chest on the table and sat to Elina's right, eyeing her curiously.

"Your Highness?" the nurse said.

"I thought you might like to oversee my king preparing my tonic."

"Of course."

Busily Chardryn opened jars and set them out. Warrick

gave to Elina the one she needed.

Elina made a show of checking the label. "I recall you shouting at my thickheaded brute of a husband that doxweed will grow hair between my toes if he gives me too much. Say, this much?" She scooped out a full thimble of the bloodbane, dumped it into Chardryn's goblet, and pushed it toward the nurse—who sat frozen. "Will you take a sip, Nanny Char?"

The nurse's face was rigid. "My queen, whatever the barbarian has said to you—"

"Your barbarian *king*," Elina corrected coldly. "The son of a witch and healer who knows precisely what each powder in your chest is and its effects. Who knew upon our first kiss that I had been drinking bloodbane. How did you put the mark upon my back? For it certainly was not inked there. One day, it simply appeared."

Chardryn's lips pressed together.

Warrick put the blade of his axe against her neck. "Answer."

"A spellcaster in Gocea, shortly after the cursed twin of Phaira tried to steal her sister's throne. I told the spellcaster you also had a sister, and you wished to be marked as the true heir so the same could not happen to you."

"Why such a ruse? Ah, but I know. So that you might blame my uncle…and if my illness was thought magical, no one would look to you. Whereas if poison was suspected, you would be the first to fall under scrutiny."

"Poison?" Dara whispered, trembling in her chair, her

eyes wide and locked on the blade against the nurse's neck.

"These five years," Elina told her. "I am not cursed. *Never* was I cursed."

Fire filled Dara's gaze and she sat up straight. "Why would you do such?" she spat at the nurse before hunching down and shooting a contrite look at Elina. "Forgive me, my queen. I only—"

"Asked what I would have next. Why?"

With shaking hands, the nurse pushed the poisoned goblet aside. "My family have ever been loyal retainers to Aleron royalty. Serving the throne is all we have ever done. All we have known. We have no home but the palace. And Soren told me that he would kill them all if I did not comply."

Elina's brows drew together in a frown. "Why did you not tell me? I would have found a way for them to leave."

"Leave the palace?" The nurse appeared affronted by the suggestion. "And do what? And *be* what? Nothing."

The slight softening that Warrick had seen in Elina vanished. "What are you when you kill the queen you serve? Certainly not a *loyal* retainer."

"You would have died either way, child. Do you truly believe you might survive if you return? You are not strong enough to defeat him."

"Is this what you have told yourself? *You* stole my strength."

"Not bodily strength." Chardryn dismissed such a thought with a wave. "A queen has armies for that. What

I speak of is strength of will."

"You believe that is what my uncle has? No. He only has cruelty. Would you have a queen as heartless as he is?"

"I would," the nurse said firmly. "Kindness will not save Aleron from your uncle. It will not save my family. Or me."

"Will it not?" Elina's brow arched. "I will let you live, Nurse Chardryn, for I understand the choice you were forced to make. That is the limit of my kindness. Never will you return to Aleron, though *I* will. I will take my throne. I will save your family from my uncle. I will not punish them for what you did, but you will never again serve. *Your* name will be struck with shame. All will know that you betrayed your queen and instead served Soren."

"Better that you kill me," the nurse muttered.

"Which is why I will not." She paused, studying the woman. "Do you suppose I will show similar mercy to Soren? You mistake kindness for weakness. Kindness is never weak when combined with firmness of purpose— which I have never lacked. Kindness will save the people of Aleron, because it is for them I will fight. Not for the throne or for all of Aleron's gold. But because I *refuse* to let them suffer." Her throat worked. "You have known me all these years. Could you truly not believe in me?"

Chardryn would not meet her eyes. "I did not dare."

Warrick watched as the queen's mask descended over Elina's face, though she wore no paint. Concealing her hurt. Brusquely she added, "Five years you spent poisoning me at Soren's behest. How long were you sending messages to tell the assassins where to find us?"

"Since we fled your father's kingdom."

Elina laughed humorlessly. To Warrick she said, "I am finished with her."

Warrick was not. Not after what she'd done to Elina. His axe near *thirsted* for her blood. "And certain you do not wish to end her?"

"Worse than death will be facing my retinue when her false curse is revealed. She will not think me kind, then. Bind her and leave her to them."

Reluctantly he removed the axe from her neck. With stout rope, he tied her to the chair hand and foot as Elina turned to Dara.

"I leave with my husband to rid Aleron of its usurper. I would have you wait beyond a full day before leaving this tent and informing them we are gone."

"I will, my queen."

Elina glanced at Chardryn as Warrick was stuffing a gag into her mouth. "Leave her tied, even if she messes herself. You know the truth of what she's done, and I fear what she might do to keep it concealed." She gave a prepared parchment to Dara. "This is written in my hand to verify what you have heard of the poisoning, and gives orders to Serjeant Iarthil not to follow me, but to guide you all to Aleron as soon as may be. To you, and to those who have been true and served me well, I give my thanks. You will be welcomed back home. So strike for Aleron. Your queen and king and family will be waiting for you there."

Hope lit the maid's face. "You will be safe?"

"I will. Good journey, Dara."

"Good journey, Your Highness." Eyes glimmering with tears, Dara helped her into a dark traveling cloak, then watched them go with hands clasped in front of her chest.

With her hand in his, Warrick led Elina through the quiet camp. "I have already saddled Troll, so all is ready."

"Troll?" Amusement danced in her eyes. "You named him such?"

"It could not have been any other name."

Her soft laugh of agreement soon faded. They reached his mount. Yet instead of turning so that he could lift her, she clung to his arm instead.

"Warrick." Her voice was dizzy, uncertain. She put a trembling hand to her head. "I do not feel well."

His throat closed, preventing any response. She shivered despite the warmth of the morning and her cloak. His own traveling cloak was tied to the back of the saddle. He wrapped the heavy red material around her, lifted her astride. Swiftly he mounted behind her and pulled her tight to his chest.

"Sharing a horse again." Her head fell back against his shoulder. "Should we do bizarre things now?"

He could not even manage a smile. "Let us ride while you have any strength left at all."

"Less fun but more wise, Warrick." Her voice changed from teasing to grave in an instant. "I thank you for this.

And for helping me through what is to come."

He swallowed past the ache in his throat. "You are my heart," he said simply.

And rode.

ELINA the HEARTLESS

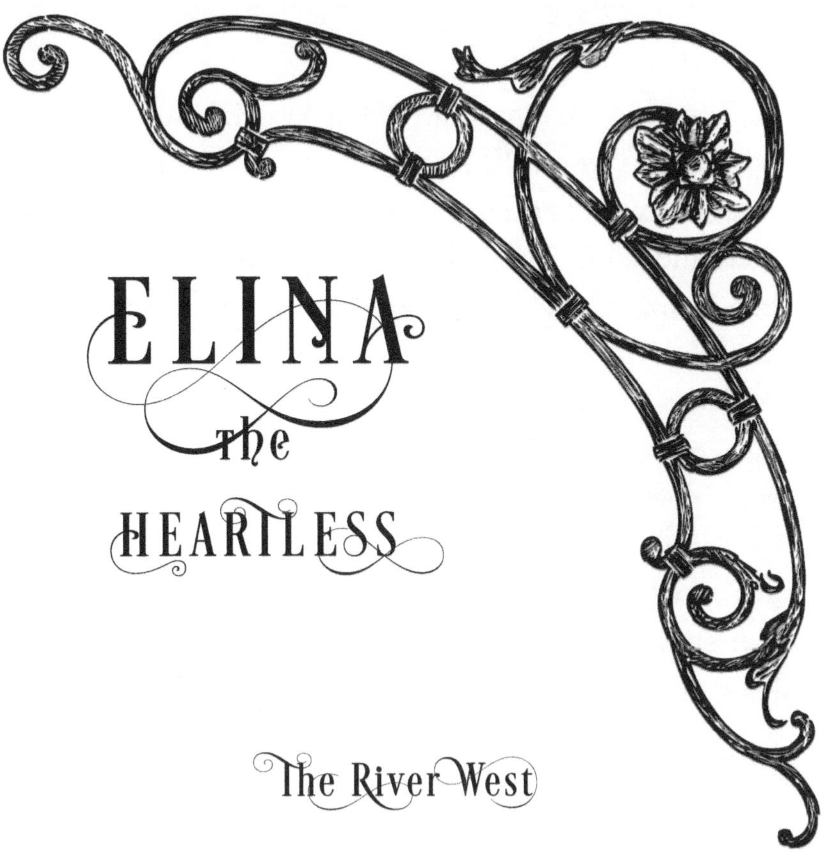

The River West

"Come, wife." Warrick strode into the cabin, wearing a grin. "You will wish to see this."

He scooped her up from the bed and Elina eagerly circled her arms around his neck. She'd taken a few steps that morn and would take her exercise again later, but could hardly leave the cabin under her own power, let alone stride quickly onto the deck of the river barge as Warrick was doing.

She cared not where they were going. Simply the warmth of sunshine upon her face and the gentle breeze of the barge's movement made their destination many times preferable to another moment spent in the cabin.

The purge had been as bad as Warrick said it would be. Perhaps worse. Elina was certain that if not for the rings, she would be dead. That fortnight had been a blur of fever and pain…but with Warrick always there. Holding her. Helping her. Urging her to stay with him, always to stay with him.

Near ten days had passed since the harrowing purge had ended, and when Elina was not sleeping the day away, she was slowly regaining her strength.

Although she could barely walk more than a few steps, already she was so much better. The constant pain and nausea were gone. She could still not eat much but only because even that small activity taxed her strength. But what she *did* eat remained in her stomach.

And Warrick's hair had grown.

For certain it had been doing so all this time—and it was still short by any standard. Yet only now, as she combed her fingers through the bristled strands at the back of his head, did she realize they had grown longer than her fingertips. No longer freshly shaved, they'd also softened. And the sun caught the short ends in such a wonderful light, making the dark tips seem near blond when she looked at them just so. The light upon his profile was even more fascinating, a stark play of angles and shadows.

"There on the riverside," Warrick said—then caught her blatantly staring at him. She'd wished to be out of her cabin to see something new…yet here she was, looking at him instead of what was around them. Just as she looked at him within her cabin.

No matter where she was, Warrick was always the finest view.

Elina flushed but flashed an unrepentant grin. She'd always loved looking at him. Had loved the thrill that the sight of his powerful body gave to hers. Yet now the thrill was…different. Deeper. She still found him meltingly appealing, yet seeing him also filled her with such happiness. To have Warrick near, to spend time with him produced a level of joy and contentment that she'd never even dreamed of.

These past days, as she'd spent longer hours awake and he'd spent them with her, it had occurred to Elina that she'd never had a friend before. Yet now she did. She'd found the finest of friends in Warrick.

And so much more.

Huskily he said, "If you wish, I will take you back to the cabin."

Oh, she wished he could. But truthfully, Elina was not yet strong enough for it. As Warrick knew very well, too.

With a sigh, she looked to the riverside. She felt the gentle kiss he placed on her ribbon-covered wrist as her gaze swept the landscape. Boulders and hills and—

Her mouth dropped open. "Is that a statue of a giant?"

"A troll. Or used to be, before it was turned to stone."

Yes, now Elina could discern how the proportions were all wrong for a giant human—the head too domed; the mouth too wide and with loose, slavering lips; the body too heavily built for its frame though packed with muscle.

Warrick's horse was truly well named, as he could also be described so.

"Why was it turned to stone?"

"The legend says that he angered Anhera."

"Oh! The giant who attempted to steal her wings?"

"That is how the legend is sometimes told. But it was a troll, not a giant."

"Perhaps she stoned both. Anhera seems to enjoy that particular method of punishment. Though the stone sickness in Galoth…" Elina shook her head. "She punished those who did not deserve it."

"She did," Warrick said grimly—then jostled her a little, as if to shake them out of their sudden solemnity. "The first time Bannin and I came this way to Galoth was before the jewels were taken. I was wandering the deck at night and saw the troll standing with the moon behind it. I had no notion that it was only stone."

Elina grinned. She could well imagine how terrifying the troll would appear. "What did you do?"

"Shouted and woke everyone, waving a torch and threatening the troll with my axe. I am still known in Galoth as Warrick the Trollslayer. And not one person has ever mistaken that name for anything but what it is—they all know me for a fool."

Elina shook with laughter, as she almost always did when Warrick spoke of his and Bannin's travels. In return, she'd told him of the courts she'd visited, their intrigues—and especially their absurdities.

Yet there was one story she hadn't heard. "When did you meet Bannin?" Nearly half a world lay between Galoth and the Dead Lands.

"Fifteen years past. Or near to that."

"Not long after leaving your clan?" Warrick had been fifteen when he'd gone—the same age as Elina when she'd left Aleron. Though unlike Elina, Warrick had chosen to leave.

"The following summer. It was in Wintermere—north of the Illwind Sea."

Elina had never been so far east, but she knew the kingdom he spoke of. "And you came upon a ghost?"

Nearly all of his adventures started in that way.

"I did. She named the prince who killed her, and when I sought her murderer, I found Bannin and other mercenaries had been hired to serve as the prince's guard. Bannin did not intend to let me past him. I did not intend to be thwarted. So we were gleefully trying to kill each other when Bannin suddenly stopped and asked me why I glowed."

"So you told him?"

"And showed him the woman's ghost. Bannin returned to the prince and killed the man himself—then announced that he would travel with me henceforth."

"As *your* guard?"

Warrick laughed and shook his head. "For a diversion,

I suspect. He said that what I did was far more interesting than guarding spoiled princes."

"I imagine he is correct."

"He had not long to judge whether it was. Only a few years later, the jewels were stolen and the stone sickness struck—and we began searching for them."

Which was the source of many more of his stories, during the years when Warrick and Bannin had not becomes thieves in truth, yet often employed the same methods in their search for Anhera's stars. She knew of no one who'd hidden under so many beds or climbed through as many windows as Warrick.

It was unfortunate he'd never made his way under her bed. They would have found each other much sooner.

"What is it?" he asked, catching her smile.

"I was thinking that while you were searching for me, I was searching for you. Though neither of us knew who we were searching for."

"It only matters that we knew when we found each other."

Eyes warm, he lifted her hand and pressed a kiss to the red ribbon around her wrist—which had not frayed a single thread or faded in color, though she'd worn it continually for nearly a month and had subjected it to frequent washings. That their vows had cast some spell onto the ribbon could not be argued against. But as they would never unmarry, that mattered less than knowing the spell also preserved the red satin, and she would never have to fear the ribbon would tatter and break.

"Shall I carry you to see *our* Troll?"

Elina nodded, and soon Warrick held her in the barge's stable. Troll's stall seemed hardly large enough for the monstrous horse. "He seems restless," she observed after feeding to him a slice of apple.

"He is. A few rounds of exercise upon the deck each day is not enough for him."

Elina thought it was not enough for Warrick, either, now that the worst of her sickness had passed. During the purge, he'd attended her faithfully. He'd likely never even considered leaving her side. Yet now the confinement seemed to be wearing on him. By tomorrow, he might be carrying her around all day simply to be active and moving.

And knowing now that he'd lasted a month in a lightless cell—though at any time he could have escaped—simply to give those enslaved families a better chance of remaining undetected until they sailed?

Never had Elina met anyone she admired more. "How much longer do we travel by river?"

"Ten days."

"And to Galoth?"

"Another fortnight."

That seemed enough time. She stroked Troll's velvety muzzle. "When I am strong enough, I will buy my own horse to ride."

Warrick scowled. "I prefer that you ride with me."

"As do I. But I wish to ride into Aleron upon my own

mount. Not while being held. Or…giving any appearance of being weak."

Weak as her mother had believed her to be. As Nanny Char had. Though she knew the nurse had been wrong, still Chardryn's words had worn away at Elina, fraying her own edges.

Understanding softened his frown. "Then we will find you a mount. Though never have I thought you weak, Elina. Not even during the worst of the purge, when you could not rise from your bed or lift your head."

Sweet tears clogged her throat. Thickly she asked, "Will you set me on my feet?"

Gently he did, then steadied her with his hands at her waist. At a crook of her finger, he bent his head. She rose onto her toes to meet him, a soft kiss that gradually deepened until Elina was bearing none of her own weight, for he'd lifted her against his chest to better take possession of her mouth.

When she broke away, breathless, she had to know—"Do you still taste the bloodbane?"

He shook his head. "Only your sweetness."

The sweetness was Warrick's. He kissed her lips again, then her ribbon.

Her pulse raced dizzily. Exhausted from one kiss. "I would like to spend more time kissing each day," she proposed. "Just as I walk a few steps more each day. I will build up my stamina…until I can ride a horse alone."

Warrick chuckled against her lips before tenderly

stealing another kiss. "And also ride me."

"Precisely," she laughed and threw her arms around his neck. "I *must* regain my strength. Our wedding night still awaits!"

"Then we will kiss more." His rumbling murmur against her ear sent shivers over her skin. "So that I might also build up stamina, though in my tongue."

"By all means," she agreed, breathless again. "Talking will not be enough. Only kissing."

Because it was quite necessary for her own sanity and health to keep Warrick's tongue very, *very* strong.

WHEN THEY LEFT THE RIVER barge, Elina wasn't yet able to ride on her own. Within a few days, however, she purchased a horse—though she could only ride alone in short jaunts. They often stopped to rest along the way, with Elina stumbling down out of the saddle, exhausted and aching.

At least making camp each night with Warrick was a much easier affair. Meat was cooked from a snare that he taught her to set. Bread and cheeses were easily purchased at the villages they passed through, fruits and berries collected along the way.

To sleep, they shared Warrick's bedroll—and within it, they kissed so much that Elina had to purchase a milker's balm to soothe her chapped lips.

Sitting at their campfire that night, Elina watched Warrick skin a rabbit while he watched her apply the balm with a fingertip.

"That will not be needed when I begin spreading my kisses all over you again."

Or when she began kissing *him* all over. The thought rendered the fire too warm. Restless, Elina rose and moved nearer to him, stopping beside his axe, which he'd propped head-down against the same fallen log he sat upon.

She gripped the chain and grunted—it was too heavy for her to lift more than an inch off the ground. Certainly too heavy to swing. Disappointment filled her, but she attempted to laugh it off. "I was having a wonderful dream of killing Soren myself."

Warrick did not laugh. "Every morning and night, pick it up and lift it as high as you can. At each meal, pick it up again. By the time we reach Aleron, you will be strong enough to swing it."

Hope replaced the disappointment. "Truly?"

He nodded and continued preparing the rabbit for the spit. After a moment, he looked to her again. "Why do you stare at me like that, wife?"

Because he believed in her. There'd been no hesitation in him. He'd expressed no doubt whether she could become strong enough. He simply advised her on how to accomplish what she wanted to do.

"Do not move, my king." It emerged thickly, from a throat swollen with emotion. She went to him where he sat upon the log, his knees comfortably spread and his boots flat upon the ground. Elina stepped into the space between his feet, crowding close enough that Warrick sat back and spread wide his arms, one hand holding the bloodied rabbit and the other just bloody—making certain the mess didn't touch her.

Confusion creased his brow. "Elina—"

She leaned in—kissing his mouth, his jaw, his neck. His chest.

"Elina." More hoarsely now. "Let me wash and touch you."

That did not sound like something Elina wished him to do at that particular moment. Kneeling, she slicked her tongue over his nipple, pleased by the way it tightened. Pleased by his flavor, salt and skin.

With open-mouthed kisses, she licked her way down his abdomen, which was heaving now with the great breaths he took. Oh, but she liked so well his body's reaction to her.

Just as she liked that he always wore such easily discarded clothing. Simply by unbuckling the belt that hid his navel from her questing tongue, Elina bared the rest of him, too.

She looked up at him over the length of his jutting erection. His eyes were molten, the carcass near crushed to a pulp in his effort not to touch her. And he seemed beyond words, for when she took hold of his rigid cock, he made *such* a deep and growling sound that she felt it reverberate within her own flesh. Recalling how he'd stroked his fist over his shaft until he spilled upon her belly, she began to work him the same way, though it required both of her hands.

The muscles in his thighs and stomach became steel. His breath hissed through clenched teeth.

"I think often of how this will feel inside me." She rubbed his throbbing flesh against her cheek. "When I heft your mighty weapon, my king, do you think me strong enough to take you?"

His tortured groan seemed to wrap chains of pleasure around her skin, drawing it up tight and hot. She hadn't known how blissful pleasing him would be. Yet now that she knew, likely much more time would be spent on her knees.

She turned her head and gave to his shaft an open-mouthed kiss.

Warrick's body jerked, his stomach flexing. "Elina." Swallowing her name, so deep. He heaved out more words, all a low rumbling groan. "Your mouth."

Never had she seen him so undone. So unable to speak. And near destroyed when she opened her lips over the thick crown and sucked him in. Only the head, yet he let go a great shout and his hips rolled, again, again, his eyes closed and now words tumbling from him.

"If you do not— I am near… Elina! You must—"

His shaft pulsed under her tongue. His seed exploded into her mouth. Elina coughed as a spurt hit the back of her throat. By reflex, she spit it back out.

Warrick choked on a laugh even as his cock bobbed

and twitched, more spend spilling down his shaft. "You will kill me, woman. Or ruin me. Never have I come so quickly. When I finally take you, for certain I will need to jerk my cock first. Else I will not last a moment."

Well pleased, Elina rose and straddled his lap. Warrick still laughed at himself even as she kissed him. Smiling, she lay her head against his shoulder and pressed her palm over his still-pounding heart.

His amusement quieted to a chuckle. "Can you feel anything within there? You have stolen my heart, wife. Nothing inside is left to beat."

"My heartless husband," Elina mused. "I am heartless now, too."

Warrick's laughter stopped. His entire body stilled. "What do you say?"

"It is selfish of me, but when I thought of the prophecy beyond felling my uncle, my hope was only that *I* would be loved. And when I met you, I looked forward to the pleasure to be had. But I had not thought to please you in return, though I was glad you seemed to enjoy everything you did to me. And I never thought that I might love in return." She met the darkness of his eyes. "But I do, Warrick. So very much."

She had not even a moment to draw breath before Warrick's mouth was on hers, hungry and deep. His bloodied hands came up as if to bury themselves in her hair.

Abruptly he stopped, breath gusting over her lips. "I must wash. Will I have you this night?"

Body humming with happiness, Elina nodded. "We will have each other."

"Then I will feed you after." He tossed the rabbit aside. "Hie to our bed, wife—or I will take you where I find you."

That was a promise she would take advantage of another time. Heart pounding, she hurried to the bedroll, dragging off her boots and tunic and trousers. A barbarian she'd become, too, because she tossed them aside without a care for where they lay. Her only care was where *she* would lay.

On her back, this time. Elina had not the strength to ride him for long, and the memory of him grunting and grinding between her thighs on their wedding night was one she revisited often in her mind. Hastily she arranged herself on the deep, soft furs of his bedroll and awaited her husband's return.

It was not long. Her breath caught. Warrick strode toward her wearing only rivulets of water, as if he'd scrubbed all over, not just washed his hands. He scraped his palms over his short hair and flicked away the drips, his gaze hot upon Elina's naked form as it journeyed from her toes to her eyes, lingering on the pink flesh that she offered as invitation between her opened thighs.

"You are beautiful, my wife." His hand wrapped around his cock and stroked, bringing his satiated flesh to full hardness again. "You are certain?"

Teasingly Elina drifted a fingertip down over her chest, circling the tightening peak of her breast. "I have never been more certain of anything, my husband."

A smile playing around his firm mouth, he knelt between her thighs, spread wantonly wide. Leaning in, he wet the head of his cock by slicking it through her drenched slit—his own tease, she was soon to learn, when instead of filling her with a thrust, he braced his elbows beside her shoulders and bent his mouth to her lips.

"I lovingly submit to you my heart, my flesh, and my seed, O Radiant Queen."

A laugh burst from her. "It is truly a *terrible* proposal! But one that must be said."

"One I will never regret accepting." Reaching for her hand, Warrick entwined their fingers—just as they had been entwined when they'd spoken their vows. He kissed the ribbon that braceleted her wrist, then pushed her arm up over her head, pinning her hand to the furs. "Will this be our wedding night, my wife?"

"No," she said softly, touching her jeweled fingers to his firm mouth. "As painful as that day became and the many tears I shed, I would never trade a moment of that Midsummer for another. I would never rewrite a single second I've spent with you. *And,*" she added with a grin before she could become too maudlin, "I would not have our hands bound until dawn again. Much better to touch you with two."

"Much better," Warrick agreed—though the huskiness of his reply suggested that he had not been unaffected by the rest of her speech. As did the way he kissed her, slow and sweet.

Yet he also wasted not a moment putting both hands to use. The first to clasp her nape, anchoring her in place for his deepening kiss, the other to roam where he wished.

What he apparently wished was to please her or torture her or both—stroking his fingers over her breasts, teasing and pinching her nipples. All the while devouring her mouth with kisses that were wet and slow and devastating. Yet she could not please and torture him in return, for she could only clutch his arms and his shoulders, and the frustration of not touching him now that she knew the joy of it was wound ever tighter by his fingers and tongue.

It was almost a relief when his hand abandoned her breasts to explore the plane of her stomach, to grip her ass and grind her against his rigid arousal. For it was *so* good, yet not so maddeningly overwhelming, and her thoughts were almost coherent again.

Until his roaming hand slipped between her thighs.

"So wet," Warrick groaned, breaking the kiss to breathe hotly against her mouth, his eyes half closed as if he were nearly overcome simply by the slickness of her arousal against his fingers. "Elina."

Then he was kissing her again, sending her spinning into a madness of ecstasy between the stroke of his tongue into her mouth and the circling of his thumb around her clit—then his finger pressed into her, rubbing together with the slide of his thumb, and she cried out when it became *so* much.

Warrick dragged his mouth from hers. "Hurts?" he

asked raggedly, his gaze hot on her face.

"No!" Near sobbing, she twisted beneath him. "Please. Please, please. Warrick!"

"Let it come, wife." He growled into her ear. "You're so tight. So strong. So beautiful. Let me feel you come."

His words seemed to join with his hand, shoving her into a spiral of bliss. Her body locked as she shattered, screaming into his neck, holding him close.

"Elina, my wife, my heart. You came so good," he groaned. "Now I wish for you to do it again."

Surely she could not. She was still quivering when his finger slipped from inside her, and his mouth began the same roaming journey as his hand.

And she *could* come again. She could, as his tongue made her cry out again and again, until she was a limp and liquid mess upon his furs. He rose up over her to take her mouth in another kiss. She tasted herself upon his lips, felt the heavy weight of his erection pressing into her belly, and everything inside her tightened in anticipation.

Warrick cupped her face. "The stars, Elina."

Her mind was so blissed, she knew not for a moment what he meant. Then she smiled and tugged the jewels from her fingers—feeling the oddness of their missing weight after two years of never removing them.

Yet no fear did she feel. She trusted him. She loved him.

Some undefinable emotion passed through Warrick's eyes before he kissed her again, hard, deep.

Then he braced himself over her on one straightened

arm, gripping his swollen shaft and slicking the head through her cleft. His voice was a thick rasp. "Watch me take you, wife."

Barbarian. With a soft laugh, she raised her thighs alongside his flanks, opening herself fully to him. "I am the one taking *you*, husband. My body is accepting yours."

His burning gaze met hers. "And your heart?"

"Also yours," she whispered, and he pushed forward. Sudden tearing pain stiffened her muscles, clenched her teeth. "What treachery is this?"

Warrick froze. "Elina?"

"It felt so good. And now—" She squirmed, trying to ease the brutal ache within. She glanced down to see that his shaft was barely inside and a laughing gasp escaped her. "I think all the pleasure that came before must be a lie to make a woman open her thighs."

"Put on the rings," he said hoarsely and reached between them. His fingers slicked over her clit and the shifting of his weight pushed him deeper.

That was not so bad. Just a burning sting. Then only fullness and pressure and the taut stretch of her flesh when she slipped the jewels back onto her fingers.

"Better?" Warrick was shaking against her.

She nodded.

"Thank the gods," he said, and drove full deep.

Oh.

Oh.

So *much* better. Elina wasn't yet certain if it was

pleasurable but never had she imagined this closeness, this fullness. Her hands cradled Warrick's head and she drew him down for a kiss, loving the way he groaned so deep in his chest when she slicked her tongue over his each time his hips drew back and then he pressed into her again.

That was nice, too, the rubbing inside. And his face, the way he looked to be in *such* pain, but the flush of his skin and heaviness of his eyelids and the bellowing of his chest told her that he was as far from hurting as could be. She kissed him again, and his mouth was open against hers, but only breathing raggedly—as if he was lost to everything except his need to pump that thick shaft between her thighs.

Her hands smoothed down over his sweat-slick shoulders. "Do you like it?"

"Like it?" A rough groan ripped from him. "Elina. Your cunt is so tight. And so warm." Warrick hung his head and pushed deep again. "I will not last."

"It matters not. Only that you take your pleasure while you are inside me, my king."

Warrick paused, peering down at her face. Then he tucked his hand between them again.

"Oh." A shuddering breath escaped her. Everything was so sensitive, so stretched, that the glide of his fingers over her clit felt almost as if it were his tongue and he'd been licking her for hours and she was so near to coming again.

And now inside her— She gasped and gripped the

arm braced beside her shoulder. "Warrick!"

"Like that." He began to move again, not pumping his hips but grinding between her thighs, stirring that thickness within her, so that it was rubbing and rubbing and rubbing, and it felt as if every nerve inside her had become as exquisitely, painfully sensitive as the slick bud he was still stroking. "Look how you've taken all of me, Elina. I'm full deep. And never have I imagined such a cunt, so wet and warm. So ready to fill with my seed."

Her inner muscles clenched and she cried out, her hips beginning to tilt and grind with him.

"Do you feel me inside you, wife?" He kissed her roughly, deeply, pulling back to push back in—and Elina knew not what had changed but that motion now made her back arch, and her toes curl, and inside her everything was tight and aching and it was wonderful and she needed more. "Do you feel me fucking you?"

"Yes! Oh gods." The pressure within was increasing, as if he were becoming bigger and bigger but though he was thick, so thick, it was pleasure that he was filling her with, pushing it deeper and deeper with every thrust, deeper than her cunt, until it was filling all the rest of her, too—blinding her, stealing her breath, erasing every thought except that she always needed him inside her or she would never survive. "It's good, Warrick! It's so good."

"Then take me, wife." His hand left her clit to grip her ass, lifting her higher, higher. Grunting, he surged harder, his movements more erratic now, words tumbling from him, of the grip of her cunt, the wetness, how he needed her, how he loved her, how he couldn't hold on.

Coming undone again. But inside her.

That realization hurtled her over the edge and she screamed against his throat, moving with him as all the pleasure he'd pushed inside her unleashed in a torrent through her flesh, clutching and pulling and shaking against him.

He groaned, a ragged tortured sound from low in his chest, his fingers digging into her ass, his cock pushing deep again and pulsing, pulsing within her. Releasing his seed, while he shook and kissed her again, wet and long.

Then he buried his face in her neck, his shuddering body still braced over hers, his hips still slowly stirring between her thighs. As if he would not stop until he'd given her every last drop of his seed.

Elina would happily take it. Wrapping her legs around him, she held him closer, and kissed his hair as he'd so often done to hers. "Are you alive, husband?"

"I am not."

"A pity. I'd hoped to do that again soon. But maybe… like a beast."

"Like pigs?"

She burst out a laugh before swatting his back. "You cannot tease me with that forever!"

"I can." Warrick lifted his head. "I *will*."

The intensity of that statement took her breath away— as did the way he gazed upon her face. Heart suddenly overflowing, she whispered, "Forever?"

"Forever," he said, and bent to kiss her again.

WARRICK the GLOWING

Galoth

HIS QUEEN WAS QUITE DETERMINED TO SLEEP THROUGH the morning—and despite his claims of heartlessness, never had his chest seemed so full. Warrick lay at her side, his weight braced on his cocked elbow as he studied her face. Those expressive eyebrows, at rest while she slept. Her soft lips, still rosy and swollen from his kisses. Her sweet freckles, greater in number now that she no longer traveled under a covered carriage. He wanted to kiss every one.

He leaned to murmur in her ear. "Are you awake, wife?"

"I am not," she mumbled.

"A pity. You will leave me to break my fast alone." He

touched a berry to her closed mouth, making certain that the juice painted her lips. "Though I do not mind having these all to myself."

Her tongue darted out to taste. Her eyes flew open, alight with pleasure. "That's a cap berry!"

"It is," he confirmed, and tossed the purple berry into his mouth.

"What are you doing?" Her lips pursed and her eyebrows drew together in the severest reproof. "You're eating it wrong."

"Am I?"

"Let me show you." She sat up, her hair wild and the covers sliding down around her hips, baring her breasts. "They are called cap berries for good reason. You must…"

Quickly she plucked a berry from the bowl he'd balanced on his upraised knee and capped her fingertip. She continued with more berries until her slender fingers were all topped, and then wiggled her fat purple fingertips at him.

"Now it is best to chase someone and threaten to touch them with juicy berry fingers. So you should run."

"But I do not fear your juicy berry fingers."

"You are no fun." Her nose wrinkled and she bestowed upon Warrick an adorable pout before grinning up at him. "So we skip to the best part. When you are done chasing, you just—"

One by one, she sucked the berries from her fingertips, her eyes sparkling with her laughter.

Solemnly he said, "That is not how we would eat cap berries in the Dead Lands."

Her eyebrows flicked upward, questioning and teasing. "Do cap berries even grow in the barren wasteland of the Dead Lands, my king?"

"They do not." When she snickered, he tumbled her gently onto her back. "But if they did, we would eat them thusly."

Warrick capped her small nipple with a berry.

"Oh!" Upon that exclamation, Elina caught her breath, her body stilling, her skin flushing.

He capped her other nipple, then bent his head. The berry burst under pressure from his tongue, the dark juice spilling down the curves of her breast. Elina's fingers curled into the furs when he drew the smashed berry into his mouth along with the tight bud it covered. She made a sound low in her throat, her hips moving restlessly as he suckled and teased—then gasped for breath when he released her and moved to her other breast.

"Warrick!"

"I know it, wife," he soothed. "I have left a mess of berry juice all over your delicious little tit. I will soon return to lick it clean, but first I wish to have more of my breakfast."

She gave a choked laugh, then clasped her hands to his head as he burst the second berry with his tongue. "Make certain that you do a thorough job of the cleaning, barbarian."

Warrick made utterly certain. Placing berries where

he wished, he made a serving dish of her belly, her clit, her lips. Then he returned to lick and suck and kiss, until all that flowed over his tongue was his wife's own sweet juices, and it was his head that was near smashed between her thighs as she came.

Her body was still quivering when he rose up to claim another leisurely taste of her mouth. "Can you take my cock again, wife? I will use my hand"—for the second time that morn—"if you are sore."

"I can take you." Languidly she wrapped her legs around his hips, both invitation and demand. Her eyes were half-closed, as if pleasure and passion weighed down her thick lashes. "I wish to feel you inside me again."

To hear such from her nearly made him spend. Groaning, he told her, "I have thought of nothing but how well you took me, Elina." His cock was as molten steel as he fitted the blunt head to her small opening. "Nothing but the feel of this hot cunt squeezing me so tight."

As it did again. He watched her pink flesh part around his swollen shaft as he pressed inward. *So soft and warm.* A strangled noise came from Elina's throat when he breached her entrance, then a cry when he shoved deep. Her body enclosed his aching length in a slick velvet grip, and it was all Warrick could do to remain still, kissing her berry-flavored mouth until her clutching sheath adjusted to the girth and depth of his possession.

When her hips tilted, as if seeking more, his already tenuous control began to unravel. He gave to her another deep thrust, her cunt sucking his full length on the draw and welcoming him home on the push. His arms braced beside her head began to shake, so easily did the exquisite feel of her steal his strength. Grasping desperately at some semblance of restraint, Warrick dropped his forehead to her shoulder before he tasted his way up her neck to growl into her ear.

"So *wet*, woman." Another endless thrust, and a groan ripped from his chest when Elina trembled and clenched around his invading shaft. "So snug. Your little cunt barely stretches enough to take me." Near delirious with the ecstasy of her inner walls stroking every inch of his cock, he sank deep again. "Is this how you wished to feel me inside you? You wished to be filled and fucked?"

"Yes!" Her panting breaths took on a frantic, sobbing hitch. "Please, Warrick! *Harder.*"

A command that his unraveling brain was all too happy to heed. He surged into her silken channel in powerful drives, settling into a relentless rhythm that sent his own need spiraling, higher, tighter. She was giving the deepest part of herself to him—hot, wet—yet he needed more, needed to feel her come, needed to see her face, needed to hear her scream.

His wife, his queen.

Teeth clenched with effort, he lifted his head and his heart near flung itself from his chest. With her back arched, as if offering up berry-reddened nipples atop breasts that bounced with every rough thrust, her fingers digging into his biceps and her hair rubbed into a tangle behind her head, Elina seemed utterly lost to her bliss—yet those silver eyes were locked on his face. As if watching him gave to her as much pleasure as his cock did.

So beautiful…and all his.

Heart pounding, Warrick levered back, pulling her hips with him so that his weight was better braced upon his knees and her thighs draped over his. Slowing his pace, he watched the glistening slide of his shaft into the slippery velvet of her cunt, her frame still so slim from her illness that the depth of his penetration was marked by a slight bulge beneath her flesh. Fascinated by the sight, he pressed his fingers to the evidence of his presence within her, feeling his movement from inside and out.

One day, it would be his babe bulging here, instead.

That thought frayed his control again. Only by the thinnest of threads did he refrain from folding her in half and plowing his seed deep. Though that might have been what Elina wished. With her lower lip trapped between her teeth, she tossed her head, body writhing as if seeking the hard slam of his cock.

Until his thumb slicked over her clit. She jolted as if struck by lightning, her spine arcing upward, her cunt clamping down on his shaft. A wild cry broke from her and she hooked her legs around his waist to haul her lower body up, fucking herself onto his cock.

"Warrick." Eyes glazed with ecstasy, she chanted his name. Her fingers grasped the furs, then her hair, as if searching for something to hold to. As if searching for *him.* "Warrick."

"I am here, Elina." He wrapped his left arm beneath her hips, helping her fuck her cunt onto his shaft, while his right thumb rubbed and rubbed her clit. "I will *always* be here."

She made an inarticulate sound, her back bowing higher, her body shaking—then stiffening, utterly still, except for inside her exquisite cunt, where the convulsions of her inner muscles milked the length of his cock. Sucking and pulling at him, as if demanding he fill her with his seed.

No control could Warrick have after that. Mindlessly he pumped deep, deep, his orgasm as painful in intensity as it was a release, each body-wracking shudder emptying everything within.

And still he rocked against her slick heat, though his erection was softening. Elina had softened, too, curling her arms and legs around him, her tongue and lips locked with his in the softest and wettest of kisses.

Warrick shuddered over her again, then stilled. Elina broke the kiss, burying her face in his throat.

He wasn't fully surprised to hear her giggle. "What is it, wife?"

"You, husband." Her teasing voice was muffled against his skin. "You always make certain to give me every last drop of your spend."

"So I do." Though no choice was it. Her tight cunt simply wrung it from him. As he was still within her,

Warrick rocked against her again, loving her small gasp. "At least when I spill it here you cannot spit it out again."

She burst into laughter, her entire body shaking—a delicious tremble that likely squeezed another drop from his cock. Warrick rolled onto his back, taking her with him so that he could better look upon her face.

Pure happiness shone from her, bright as the sun. His radiant queen. Sitting up with her thighs straddling his hips, wearing only Anhera's stars and the red ribbon around her wrist, she reached for the bowl of berries and set it upon his chest.

She began capping her fingertips again. "How long before we reach Galoth?"

"A full year, if you always lay abed so late after a night of fucking."

Her unrepentant grin was followed by an impertinent pop of a berry into her mouth.

"I will wake you at dawn tomorrow, woman." At full arousal and ready to have her again.

She wiggled her juicy berry fingers at him. "Wake me as you did this morn and I will have no complaints. How far?"

"A day. Mayhap two. We are near the crossroads that mark the border of the realm." He laid his palm upon her thigh, and something in his touch must have conveyed the gravity of what he would tell her next, for despite her berry fingers and her nakedness, she suddenly regarded him solemnly. "Even before we reach the crossroads, we will ride past the statues of those who thought fleeing Galoth would save them. It is not easy to see. Especially the children. And within Galoth…there are so many more."

"I will be prepared." She swallowed thickly. "Somewhat."

Warrick set aside the bowl and sat up, catching her face in his hands. "You are my heart, Elina."

She smiled tremulously. "You are mine," she whispered and kissed him, tasting of berries and the sun and all the years that lay ahead of them.

So perfect. Warrick could not say the same for the rest of the world, but between Elina and him, everything was right.

And nothing was wrong.

No one person ruled over Galoth, just as no one ruled the Dead Lands. But instead of clans, independent clusters of farming villages and townships were spread over the verdant hills, and surrounded a larger city where Anhera's temple stood atop a granite rise.

The road to that city passed through several villages. For two days, Elina rode beside Warrick—until he noted the increasing attention she received, the glances and quiet exclamations from the villagers. She had not attempted to hide Anhera's stars; the sun gleamed off the jewels that graced the hand she used to hold her reins.

Though she could not be harmed, he would also not allow them to be separated. Without a word, Warrick hauled Elina out of her saddle and settled her in front of him.

A moment later, a villager ran up beside them. Cautious hope lined his face. His left arm was stone to his elbow. "Are they…?"

He did not finish, as if he could not bear to ask the question, fearing an answer that might destroy his hope.

"They *are* the Stars of Anhera," Warrick told him. "We are returning them to the temple."

The man stumbled to his knees and burst into sobs. "May the gods bless you both! The stars are found!" he cried to the others milling about, drawing cries of joy and wonder. "We march to the temple!"

Warrick held Elina closer, aware of the tears steadily dripping down her cheeks. Just as they had when she'd seen the first statues, her expression utterly stricken with horror…and guilt.

"You could not have known," he reassured her now as he had then. "A grave wrong was done to these people, yet it was not done by you. *You* are here to right it. *You* are here to end it."

She nodded yet said nothing. Mayhap unable to speak.

And the villagers *did* begin to march. A crowd gathered behind—some on foot, some on horses or in wagons, some coming closer to catch a glimpse of the rings. Affected by the outpouring of happiness and celebration, slowly Elina began to smile again, and laugh at the antics of the children who were trying to get her attention.

They were passing another statue when she abruptly

said, "You are not glowing."

Bemused, he replied, "I am not."

"I had thought that with all of the"—she gestured to the stone woman—"there would be many ghosts, waiting for a wrong to be righted. Not only for the stars to be returned, but also waiting for the person who stole the jewels to be caught. I thought all of Galoth would be a haunt."

Warrick frowned. In truth, he'd not considered it before. The horror of what had happened to everyone who suffered from the curse was enough. He'd never thought of how, after dying of the stone sickness, each person's horror might continue as a ghost.

"I know not why," he said slowly. Unless the ghosts were also locked in the stone. Or unless the stone figures were *not* dead—which was another horror altogether. "Mayhap it is a part of the curse."

Elina chin lifted. "Then let us break it."

THEY WERE NOT FAR FROM the city gates when Bannin came galloping down the road to meet them, reins looped around a hand that was fully stone to his wrist.

"Warrick the Trollslayer!" Bannin shouted the greeting, laughing merrily as he pulled his horse to a halt—and Warrick had never seen the big warrior so *giddy* before. Not even when drunk. Nor could he mistake wild hope in the man's face. "You have the jewels? Or do these good people follow you in anticipation of seeing you frighten another troll?"

"My wife, Queen Elina of Aleron, has returned the Stars of Anhera to Galoth," Warrick told him. When Bannin's auburn brows shot skyward, his startled gaze moving from Elina's face to the rings on her hand, Warrick shook his head to delay the questions he knew would come. "I will explain all later."

"Good enough. Come!" Bannin spun his horse around. "Let us race to the temple. Not another moment will we suffer under this curse. I hope that giant shamble of a stallion can run?"

Fast enough that they beat Bannin to the city gates. Yet there they had to slow, for the streets were filled with people awaiting the stars' return, many of them reaching out to touch Warrick's and Elina's legs as they rode past, then joining the crowd who followed behind.

Bannin escorted them through the city, until they arrived at the granite mount upon which Anhera's temple stood. Though no tall mountain, the rise could only be scaled on foot. Steep, twisting stairs led from the base of the mount to the doors of the temple.

Elina was eyeing those stairs with trepidation.

Warrick recalled her determination to ride into Aleron on her own horse, so that none of her people would think her weak. No doubt she had no wish for the people of Galoth to think the same of Aleron's queen. "I will carry you if you cannot reach the top," he said to her quietly. "There will be no shame in it."

She nodded as if in agreement, but by the lift of her chin, Warrick knew she would reach the temple on her own two feet.

Yet the decision was soon taken out of her hands. Though she climbed steadily, such a crush of people followed so closely behind—with those lower on the stairs pushing the ones ahead faster—that she was frequently jostled and nudged. They had not gone a hundred steps before Warrick knew he would either have to carry her to prevent a trampling or shove back at those climbing the stairs after her, though they in turn were being shoved by those behind.

"Elina," he implored quietly.

She met his gaze, face flushed and chest heaving. Unable to speak a word past her labored breaths, she merely nodded.

Warrick swept her up—not against his chest, where he wished to hold her secure, but seating her upon his shoulder.

"I am no golden sedan chair, my queen," he said to her, climbing again. "Yet I hope I am a fair substitute."

He felt her laugh. Yet if she would have replied, she still had no breath for it. Nor did Bannin, puffing alongside them.

Warrick squeezed her thigh and tilted his head to indicate his friend. "Do you think that old shamble of a warrior can run?"

"Old!" Bannin huffed in outrage, his sweating face as

red as his hair. "I'll have…you…know, Troll…slayer—"

Whatever Bannin would have Warrick know, he'd have to catch up to say it. Warrick surged ahead of Bannin's tortured groan, and was quickly followed by the sound of the other warrior's thumping steps.

Yet this was no race. Warrick wanted to give Elina a few moments at the top before they were surrounded by the crowd coming in their wake. For if the statues along the road were difficult, they were nothing to what awaited her in Anhera's courtyard—the sheer number of them who'd dragged their stone limbs up the stairs to beg the goddess for mercy in their final moments, their bodies still bowed in supplication. Or the ones who had been hauled up after the transformation was complete—many of them young, their statues daily tended to and dressed by their loved ones. All brought here in the hope that, with Anhera's own statue looking upon them, she would relent and let no one else suffer from the curse.

Yet she had not relented.

That goddess's tall granite figure stood in front of the enormous stone tree that served as her temple. With a feathered cowl draped over much of her face, little of Anhera's features could be seen beyond a thin mouth and narrow chin. Behind her arched stone wings, caught in the moment before flight. Her figure was as emaciated as a corpse, her narrow chest and concave stomach bare. A skirt beaded with strings of fox skulls fell in a column from bony hips to her clawed toes.

Her right arm was outstretched, palm up and fingers open. Before the theft of the stars, that arm had hung at her side, as the left one still did.

Anhera's priestess approached, near fully concealed by her raven-feathered cloak. Warrick felt Elina trembling as he set her down, though whether from the force of her emotions or fatigue from the steps she'd climbed, he didn't know—and it mattered not at all. Her shoulders went back, her spine stiffened, and he saw her again as she'd been in the prison. Though not arrogant and haughty. Instead a woman who would muster every bit of her strength to do what must be done.

She slipped the rings from her fingers and placed them in the priestess's palm. Dark wings unfurled behind the cloaked woman—wings made of more shadow than feather, and more magic than flesh.

Elina reached for his hand, entwining their fingers. Despite the gathering crowd, it was utterly quiet as a sweep of shadowed wings lifted the priestess into the air. She carried the stars to Anhera's outstretched hand and slid the rings—many times larger now—onto the goddess's taloned fingers.

Warrick found himself holding his breath. Then it was knocked from him as Bannin suddenly embraced him, thumping his back.

Thumping his back with a hand of flesh.

Cries rose around them, rising and rising until they became a roar of voices. A laughing Bannin grabbed

Warrick's face before smashing a kiss to his mouth, then twirled back, lifting his arms over his head and howling with glee. Elina was laughing, too, and clutching his hand ever tighter. Suddenly she stilled and her mouth dropped open.

Tears gleamed in her eyes. "Look."

At the supplicating statues…no longer statues, but again flesh and blood. Disoriented but moving—and now swarmed by those helping them rise, then sobbing and embracing.

Bannin returned from his twirl, his happy tears streaming down his face. He clapped Warrick's shoulders and shouted, "Warrick the Cursebreaker!"

Elina grinned up at him. "It is a good name. He broke my curse, too."

"Did he?" Bannin's brows rose. He gave Warrick a sly glance.

Warrick knew that look. With a pained sigh, he shook his head. He'd forgotten all about the plan to break a curse with his cock. "I will explain later."

Bannin barked out a laugh before abruptly sobering and looking to Elina. "It must be asked—did you steal the jewels? Or know who did?"

"I did not. I do not." She spread her hands. "They came to me two years past, when I was traveling through Talladale."

"A raven dropped them into her lap. No jest," said Warrick, when Bannin gave to him a disbelieving glance.

"I had not known what they were. Not until Warrick told me. All credit for their return belongs to him."

Bannin knew enough of the world to know that was untrue. There were many who would not have relinquished the jewels so easily. And as if to contradict her assertion of deserving no credit, a woman holding an infant came to Elina, near incoherent in her gratitude. "My baby… she was— You, never enough. Anything you wish, I will. Anything for you."

Elina's gaze flicked to his, and Warrick saw again her horrible guilt. Yet his queen would never be ungracious, and her smile was genuine as she stroked the child's cheek with a gentle forefinger. "I wish for nothing except that you love and cherish this little one for many years to come. I was very happy to help—and I am so very happy for you both."

Another came to thank her. Another. She seemed more stricken by each one, though Warrick doubted anyone else could recognize her distress. No one else would understand the straightness of her shoulders and stiffness of her spine. His wife was at the very end of her strength, though now it was her emotional strength and not the physical. Instead of smiling, she likely wished to burst into tears.

Warrick well knew how undeserved the gratitude for righting a wrong could feel. He'd been thanked many times in this same way—beyond mere recognition of a simply righted wrong and accompanied by offers of gold, favors, and blood obligations. All made him leave a place as quickly as could be. Yet Elina must feel the additional burden of accepting thanks for a wrong that she felt *she* had done to these people, by possessing the jewels for so long.

He pulled Bannin near, spoke low. "She is overwhelmed. I will take her to the inn near the mill. This time ought to be for Galoth—those who suffered and grieved, and who now are reuniting."

"And I must go to Helana and Ouin." Then Bannin grinned and he boomed out, "But we will feast this night! Be prepared to drink a thousand toasts to your name, Cursebreaker. And, of course, to the lovely Queen Elina."

She laughed as he bowed deeply before her, then laughed all the more when he bent over her hand and gallantly kissed her fingers.

Lips against her skin, he eyed Warrick over her knuckles. "Look how he is ready to take that axe to my head merely for touching your hand. Some friend he is, yes?"

"He is." Elina lifted her gaze to his. "Truly the best of friends—and will be the best of kings."

Bannin's brows rose, as if this were the first time he'd grasped the full ramifications of Warrick calling a queen his wife. "I *will* hear this story later?"

"You will," Warrick told him. "This night, at the inn's tavern."

For there was part of the story that Elina had yet to hear, too.

...

No chance did Warrick have to meet with Bannin at the tavern. After securing a bedchamber, Elina cried in Warrick's arms until she fell asleep. There he held her, listening to her gentle breaths and the ever-growing noise of celebration throughout the city. When she awoke, night had fallen. Moonlight through their open shutters revealed the peace she'd found in her sleep, her eyes no longer stricken with guilt. From the inn's courtyard came music and laughter, and it was to those jubilant sounds that Warrick lovingly fucked her in their soft bed—the first proper bed that he'd taken her in—and did not stop until he'd made her come on his fingers and tongue and cock.

Only then did they leave their chamber to seek his friend.

To accommodate the crowds spilling out of the tavern, tables and lanterns had been moved into the courtyard. Despite the number of revelers who danced and drank, Bannin stood taller than most and was easily spotted—especially when he was whirling about while holding a happily squealing boy above his head.

"That is Ouin," Warrick said to Elina, then gestured to a tall red-haired woman dancing closely with a one-armed man. Lightness filled Warrick's chest to see him. "Bannin's sister, Helana, along with her husband, Aven."

"The husband who was stone?"

"She has not taken another," said Warrick, then grinned

when Elina pulled him into the midst of the dancers.

She had been too ill to dance after their wedding. Yet she wasted no time now joining Bannin and Helana, though her eyes were only for Warrick. She draped her arms around his neck and kissed his mouth before twirling away, and soon the sway of her hips was tempting him to drag her up to their bed again.

"Oick! Not the beard, boy!"

Bannin staggered to a stop beside him, face flushed with the dance and ale. A giggling Ouin was handed over to Helana, who gave to her brother a narrowed stare before kissing Warrick's cheek.

"There are not enough thanks, Trollslayer. You are already a brother to him"—she elbowed Bannin in his gut—"but you are family now to all of us."

Bannin hissed to him loudly, "She wants another brother so that she can ask you to mind Ouin while she and Aven *reunite*. Oof!"

While Bannin rubbed his battered stomach, Helana smiled sweetly at them both and carried Ouin back to where her husband waited at a table.

"You are minding the boy tonight?"

"I am. Likely I'll play nursemaid for the next month. They have five years to make up for, so I will not be adventuring again soon."

"While my axe still has a sorcerer to fell."

Elina danced up to his side, eyes sparkling. "Look at Ouin. What did I say of how to eat those berries?"

The boy sat on the table, waving berry fingers in Helana's face, while she pretended to cringe in horror—until Aven stole a berry from the boy's thumb with a quick nip of his teeth, then made Ouin scream with tickles.

"You wish for me to tickle you?"

Her brow arched as if considering. "Perhaps that, too."

"Warrick tells me that you next travel north to kill your uncle?" Bannin asked.

"We do. Soon, I think," Elina said, and Warrick nodded his agreement. Best not to wait.

Bannin huffed out a laugh. "That was not your original plan, brother."

"Much changed."

"I see it did. For the better—and prettier." Grinning, he glanced at Elina again and clapped Warrick's shoulder. "You can trust this one to fell any tyrant. Or, apparently, to break any curse." With that, he raised an ale over his head and bellowed, "Let us drink to Warrick *the Cursebreaker!*"

"Elina the Cursebreaker," Warrick said as the courtyard resounded with cheers, and she gave to him a look that warned him she'd rather not be known as such.

Then she snickered. "Your legend soon looks to be secure. And I like your friend very well."

Warrick groaned to see Bannin climbing onto a table, sloshing his ale as he shouted for attention.

"My friends! My friends! Listen here! Warrick has said he will tell the story of how the Stars of Anhera were returned to this land—and what a tale I expect it to be, as the torch-wielding Trollslayer becomes a cock-wielding Cursebreaker!" Shouts of laughter and approval came from the gathering crowd, with Bannin nodding his encouragement before holding up his hand. "The beginning of this story I was witness to myself. Still ripe from a Torrathian prison he comes to me, saying he's met a haggard gold queen wearing the stars. 'Let us go take them from her,' said I—and said he, 'The jewels cannot be taken from her, but a virgin is she…and she asked me to become her king. But if she wishes for a deflowering poke, she will first have to take off the rings!'"

The whistles and cheers in response felt as if they might split Warrick's skull. A great ache took up place in his chest. He'd meant to tell Elina this same story tonight. Of his assumptions. Of his arrogance. Of his stupidity. He would have made her laugh at him. Then later, alone, he would have told her of his shame that he'd wronged her so badly.

He would not have told her like *this*.

"Was that truly what happened?" Elina's face was a mask and she stared woodenly ahead. "You accepted my proposal—and insisted on sharing my bed—so you could take the rings?"

"At the prison, I assumed you were the one who'd stolen them. I thought you'd cursed Galoth." Sick dread twisted through his gut. She'd crossed her arms over her chest, holding herself separate from him. Warrick could not even take her hand as he said urgently, "All was different after the pool and the mudbeast. I understood then how wrong I'd been."

"I see," she said flatly.

"Then Warrick says to me, 'Go home, Bannin the Mighty! By summer's end, I will bring to you the rings and the head of the hag queen!'—and so he did. Never let it be said Warrick the Cursebreaker does not keep his promises…though I did not think her head would still be attached! And a lovely head it is, Your Highness." Amid more laughter, he bowed to Elina before turning again to cry out, "That is another tale to be told: the story of a second curse broken by our Cursebreaker, as the horrid gold hag became a comely young queen—a queen to whom Anhera's raven delivered the Stars of Anhera, so that she might bring them to our home and end the curse of stone. Let us drink to the Radiant Queen of Aleron!"

Chants of "The Radiant Queen!" rose through the courtyard. Shoulders straight and spine stiff, Elina smiled and nodded to those nearest around them.

"Now let us hear from the ghost-talking warrior! Join me, Warrick the Cursebreaker—the story you tell will be legend!"

He cared nothing of legends. "Elina," he said desperately, for all of her had become rigid. Her body, her face, and the silvery gaze whose focus refused to fix on him. As if looking at him no longer brought her pleasure. He caught her face between his hands and something deep within his chest cracked when *still* she would not meet his eyes. "You know that none of what I believed must be done in the prison *was* done. All was overturned as soon as I understood that I was wrong."

"It must have been." She gave a mirthless laugh. "After all, my haggard gold head is still attached to my neck."

His throat constricted. "Elina—"

"Go be with your friends. Tell them the legendary story they wish to hear. How you saved me from the mudbeast and broke the false curse, exposing those who betrayed me so that we could travel west to return the rings. Tell them how it was meant to be. Tell them of the raven and the prophecy that I spoke into truth because I was so desperate to help my people and to be loved." Stepping back, she pulled her face from the embrace of his hands. "I will return to the inn."

"I will return with—"

"No! I will be well." Staring fixedly away, she said in a strained voice, "And I would not have you with me now."

He could not breathe. She did not want to be with him *now*...or always? Feeling as if she'd cleaved an axe through his chest, Warrick watched her slip through the crowd and into the inn.

A hard clap against his shoulder jolted him forward. "All is well?" Bannin asked.

Bannin. Sudden rage flooded the bleeding gash inside Warrick's chest. His hands clenched into fists, fighting the urge to turn and thrash the man. To tear his loose tongue from his mouth.

But Warrick had only himself to blame. Everything Bannin said had first spouted from Warrick's own tongue. Nor could he blame Bannin for making a jest of it all. Mistaking Elina for some haggard gold villainess *was* laughable. As had been Warrick's plan to retrieve the jewels from her.

But his friend could not know it was no joke to him. Not when Warrick knew how near he came to never seeing Elina for who she was. How near he came to losing her.

Now he might, anyway.

"What ails you, brother? Are you too parched to speak? Get this man an ale!"

A mug was shoved into his hand. But Warrick was not parched. Nor could he drink. He could not swallow anything past the ache in his throat as he pictured the mask Elina had worn. He'd seen it before. Not the gold paint, but the face beneath it—her features stiffened, as the rest of her was, yet not merely from holding onto her strength.

That was the mask she used to conceal her pain.

"Ahhh." Bannin made a drawn-out sound of understanding. "I see what's distracted you. And I'll say, I feared this might happen. Not everyone stayed as true to those lost to the curse as Helana did. Some took up another love, yet now the old loves have returned…" He blew out a lip-buzzing breath and smacked Warrick's chest with the back of his hand. "Well, go on with you. I'll tell them you have a ghost to find and a wrong to right—and you'll tell us your legend another time."

Blinking, Warrick glanced down. His archer was glowing. Though it hadn't been alight even a minute before. Which meant a new ghost was nearby…likely because someone had just been killed.

Someone nearby.

His heart seized with fear. *Elina!* was his only thought. No memory did Warrick have of plowing through the crowd outside the inn or lunging up the stairs to their chamber. She had no jewels to save her from harm. Chardryn knew the route they would take west. Her uncle's assassins were still seeking her—and she'd been pointed to and named the Queen of Aleron for everyone to hear.

Now she was alone. Unprotected.

Warrick crashed through the chamber door, scanning the floor, the bed, the privy corner.

Not there. She was not there.

Was she safe elsewhere? Had she remained down in the tavern? He knew not. He only knew that nothing would be right until she was in his arms again.

Heart pounding, he turned to find her, then pivoted sharply back toward the bed when a rivulet of crimson caught his eye.

That could not be— Elina would *not* have removed—
She had.

The red ribbon that she'd worn as a bracelet since their wedding lay on their bed. With trembling fingers, he picked up the discarded length of satin from sheets still mussed from their earlier lovemaking. His stomach heaved into his throat when he saw the cleanly sheared ends.

She'd *cut* the ribbon from her wrist.

Elina had unmarried him.

Suddenly disoriented, his every thought lost, Warrick cast his gaze about the chamber again, searching for her—his wife, the one person who could fix what had become so terribly, terribly wrong—yet he only noted what else was missing.

Her clothes. Her satchel. Her traveling cloak.

Agony rent his chest. Not just unmarried. *Gone.*

But she'd not been gone for long. Minutes, at most.

Clutching the ribbon, he charged down the stairs. Not in the tavern. The stables, then.

Relief almost staggered him to his knees. *There.* Leaving the stables, wearing his axe buckled against her back, leading her saddled horse.

"Elina!"

She didn't turn. Or even pause. Not acknowledging him—no doubt furious with him. But did his wife truly think he would let her go? Without a word? Without a fight? Or *ever*? Well, she could not ignore what was right before her.

He passed her in a few long strides and pivoted, planting his massive body in front of hers. His arms crossed over his chest, a snarl already working up through his throat that would challenge her to *try* leaving him and to see how far she would get before Warrick tossed her over his shoulder and carried her back to their bed, where they could talk and fuck through her anger as any two people who loved each other ought to.

Yet every intention wheezed from him as the sight of her face drove a stony fist into his stomach. Elina was not furious. She was not wearing her mask. She was not *anything*. Simply staring ahead, seeing nothing, her silvery eyes not even an old woman's, but simply…empty. Numb. As if too emotionally shattered to even cry.

And not registering his presence at all. She plodded forward, unseeing.

His shame and regret took a chokehold upon his throat. He raised shaking hands to catch her face, to bring her empty gaze up to meet his. "Please, Elina. Do not—"

She walked through him.

Through him. In a rush of warmth, gone as she moved on. Warrick stood unbreathing, his thoughts reeling. How—? He looked down at his empty hands. Caught sight of the glowing archer.

Because a ghost was near.

His chest emptied of air. Emptied of his heart. His vision blurred, and he would have fallen then, would have joined her where he fell, except for Elina herself and her dull, unseeing eyes.

She'd been alone. She'd been harmed. And Warrick had not saved her.

But he would help her now. What little he could do. *Nothing* could make this right.

"Elina." He caught up to her again and the tears clogging his throat roughened his voice to a low, thick rasp. "What happened to you? Who hurt you?"

"Need any help, lass?" The query came from an old man leaning up against the paddock fence, smoking a long pipe. He eyed Warrick skeptically.

Elina roused the merest bit, as if lit by a faint spark. "Which way to the road north?"

The old man pointed with his pipe. "You'll turn at the river. The wooden bridge will take you straight on to the northern way."

"I thank you," said Elina and plodded on.

Warrick stood rooted in place. Perhaps the old man could also speak to ghosts. But ghosts did not carry an axe. Or lead a horse. And her hair had not whitened.

Yet she *had* walked through him. He'd not dreamed that.

The old man snorted. With a lift of his chin, he gestured to Warrick's hand. "Cut your ribbon, did she? Declared you dead to each other and took what was hers. A cold, cold bed you'll have, barbarian."

The ribbon. The priestess at the temple had tried to stop Elina from wearing Anhera's stars, fearing what spell the magic would make of their vows. And *this* was what the magic had done—cutting the ribbon had made them as if dead to each other.

Ghosts to each other.

So she had truly not seen him. Or heard him. Yet Warrick could see and hear her.

At least it was easy to guess what would reverse the spell. Warrick's fingers felt clumsy and thick as he retied the severed ends of the ribbon. Instantly the knot he made slipped apart. In frustration, in desperation, he tried again. His knot would not stay tied.

He needed no priestess to tell him that only Elina would be able to tie the ribbon. Only she could remarry them.

Though he doubted that she would on this day. Even if she could see him. Even if she could hear him. She'd left him, intending to return home. To kill her uncle. To help her people.

And she intended to do it alone.

His blood ran cold. *Never.* Even if she did not see him, even if she never knew he was beside her, she would not face what awaited her alone. He would be there with her. At a run, he returned to the stables. Saddled his horse. And did the only thing his heart could ever allow him to do.

Warrick followed her.

ELINA *the* WIDOW

Galoth

ONWARD. NO MATTER HOW MUCH SHE WISHED TO STOP and cry. One word became a refrain in her mind.

Onward.

Onward.

Onward.

Until she reached home.

She had begun to believe her home would always be with Warrick.

Which only proved her a fool, after what she'd learned. Then she proved herself a fool again shortly after crossing the wooden bridge and starting onto the road north. Her gelding had neighed the same greeting that he'd sometimes neighed to Troll while they'd been traveling upon the road to Galoth. Oh, how her stupid heart had leapt!

But no one was behind her. No one was beside her.

So she rode through the day, not seeing anything except for the joy in Warrick's eyes that she'd once thought was the joy of seeing her face for the first time. But his only joy had been discovering the jewels on her fingers.

Then other memories assaulted her, and she could see nothing but his grim pleasure as she was about to drown. At the time, she'd believed herself mistaken. That she couldn't have seen such.

Yet she had.

She also remembered how he'd held the knife he'd used to shave his head. How tightly he'd gripped it, and her impression then that he was preparing to use it in another, more violent way.

Because he *had* wanted to. He'd wanted to use it on *her*.

Elina didn't know what had changed Warrick's mind. But he *had* intended to see her die. She understood that now.

Just as she understood that everything he'd said of loving her was a lie. Warrick had not followed her from his prison cell because his heart was hers. He'd followed for the Stars of Anhera.

And when he'd first seen her face, the world had not overturned in the way that he'd said. No. When Warrick first saw her face, he'd wanted to kill her. Then he'd decided to make her want him so badly that she would remove the jewels on her own.

How fortunate for him that she'd not been haggard and horrible but young and eager and so very *very* stupid.

By the end of the first day, Elina knew not how she even drew breath under the weight of his betrayal. The gaping wound in her chest was worse than any she'd felt before…yet she was also numb. So numb. It took all of her strength to keep her gaze fixed on the road ahead.

When darkness fell, she made camp but could not remember making a fire. Yet she must have, because she sat stupidly in front of the flames that burned a collection of sticks and twigs in a stone ring. Just the sort of fire Warrick had shown her how to build.

She laid out her bedroll. Her horse was grazing. She'd forgotten to eat.

She didn't care.

SHE COULD FEEL HIS WARMTH beside her. Could breathe in his scent. Elina wished to never rise from her bed if these were the sweet dreams she would have.

But her dreams were a lie.

She made herself eat bread with cheese. Done, she picked up Warrick's axe—the one thing she'd taken care to bring with her, though the prophecy had been proven false, too. Nothing magic about it, just a few lines scribbled by Lady Faraine that she'd paid a healer to recite. Clearly Elina hadn't spoken anything into truth. No one had loved her after laying eyes upon her face. No one's heart would compel him to follow her forever after. And this axe was not destined to fell her uncle.

And yet…she had held onto that hope for so long. It did no harm to hold onto the axe now. She would need *some* weapon to kill Soren. Why not this one?

It was not even theft. Warrick's axe was hers. He'd said it again and again. Perhaps that had been a lie, too. But he *had* said it.

Elina hefted the blade. Then stood staring down the road on which she'd come. Saw how empty it remained.

She could return to Galoth. Return and demand answers. But what might he say? He'd taken one look at her face and intended to kill her. Then he'd claimed that same moment was when he began to love her. What acceptable explanation could he give for his lies?

Surely the empty road was explanation enough. If Warrick had more to say, he would be on it. Following her. But he'd done what he'd meant to do and had returned the jewels to Galoth. Never would Elina forget *those* joyous faces. The children, running on feet that had been stone. The families joined together again, dancing and laughing and loving.

Such happiness was surely worth the price of her shattered heart.

Now she needed to bring joy to her own kingdom. Elina turned north, toward the one purpose that she had left.

Onward.

...

ALWAYS GUARDED BY KNIGHTS—AND THEN Warrick—Elina had not given much thought to the dangers of riding alone. She wore a homespun traveling cloak and displayed no wealth, which seemed enough to deter the interest of thieves or assassins. The road had never posed any other threat to her when she'd traveled with her retinue.

Yet when she spotted the three riders ahead, something about their interest in her approach sent a shiver of unease over her skin. The unease became fear as the distance between them closed and she discerned their rapacious leers.

Alone on the road with them. Far from any village. Far from any help.

She could only rely on herself.

As they neared, Elina gripped handle of her axe and laid the weapon across her lap. She must have looked quite fierce—or they could see how little she had left to lose, the bleak purpose in her eyes—because immediately one of the men raised his hands as if to show how harmless he was.

He would not even meet her gaze, staring at a point over her shoulder as he called out placatingly, "We were only looking! Who would not cast an appreciative eye upon such a right comely wife?"

"Begone from me," she spat and let the axe's chain unravel with a menacing slither. "Or I will split your skulls with one swing of my blade."

The men blanched and spurred their horses down the road. She watched them go.

No one else came.

Elina would have shared her triumph with Warrick, as she'd shared so much with him before—as a friend, a lover, a wife. And he would have praised her for her strength.

Surely it was not *all* a lie? He'd cared for her so tenderly through the purge. He'd stopped the poisoning and revealed Nanny Char's betrayal. Had he done so only to gain her trust? To separate her from her retinue and lead her to Galoth? To make her more susceptible to his seduction?

Surely he'd known there was no need for the latter. Elina had been ready to open her thighs while he was still imprisoned in his cell.

She'd only meant to use him. For her pleasure. For his axe. For her people. If he'd used her in return to break a curse, could she truly think ill of him for it?

And regardless of how she'd begun…Elina loved him now. Beyond anything. Perhaps Warrick had truly come to love her, too?

But the road behind was so very empty. And there was no one to share her triumph with. No one to share the tale of how her snare finally yielded a mangy little squirrel. No one to share the roasted meat that she only picked at.

No one to share her bed.

Though when she closed her eyes at night, she could feel him as if he were there. A whisper over her skin. His warmth at her side. In her dreams, Warrick kissed her. Said her name. Told her to tie the ribbon.

But when she awakened, the warmth fled. And there was only one thing to do then.

Onward.

THE FIRST DAYS BECAME THE first fortnight.

Every night, her dreams were filled with him.

Every day, the road behind was empty.

The Glass Mountains lay ahead.

Onward.

THEN SHE BLED.

She'd been swinging the axe at a tree when she noticed the trail of blood down the inside of her thigh, and idly wondered if she'd cut herself without realizing.

When Elina understood what it was, she almost laughed. Beyond a bit of spotting, she hadn't had her courses in years. Not since the poisoning had begun. But her body was healing. This blood meant she could carry a child.

This blood also meant she was not with child *now*.

Sudden agony split open her heart. Until that moment, Elina had not even known of the hope she'd carried within her. But Warrick had left her with *nothing*.

Nothing but dreams and lies.

The numbness shattered. The sobs erupted before she

knew they were swelling and she nearly dropped to her knees, crushed by the force of them. As if she'd drowned in that river, had sucked in water instead of the lifesaving air that Warrick had given, and now the drowning river spilled from her in tears.

And *rage*. Screaming, she struck with the axe, over and over again. Not seeing a tree but seeing her uncle, her mother, her father, Lady Faraine, Serjeant Iarthil, Nanny Char—and Warrick.

Could not one of them have loved her as she had loved them? Not *one*? Would she *always* be so…so…

Unloved.

Her arms gave out and Elina stumbled back before she slid to the ground, weeping.

She knew not for how long she cried. Eventually she would have to rise. And go onward. But though she had the strength, she had not the heart.

Until something fluttered against her hand. Eyes still blurry with tears, she only saw red. But not blood.

A ribbon.

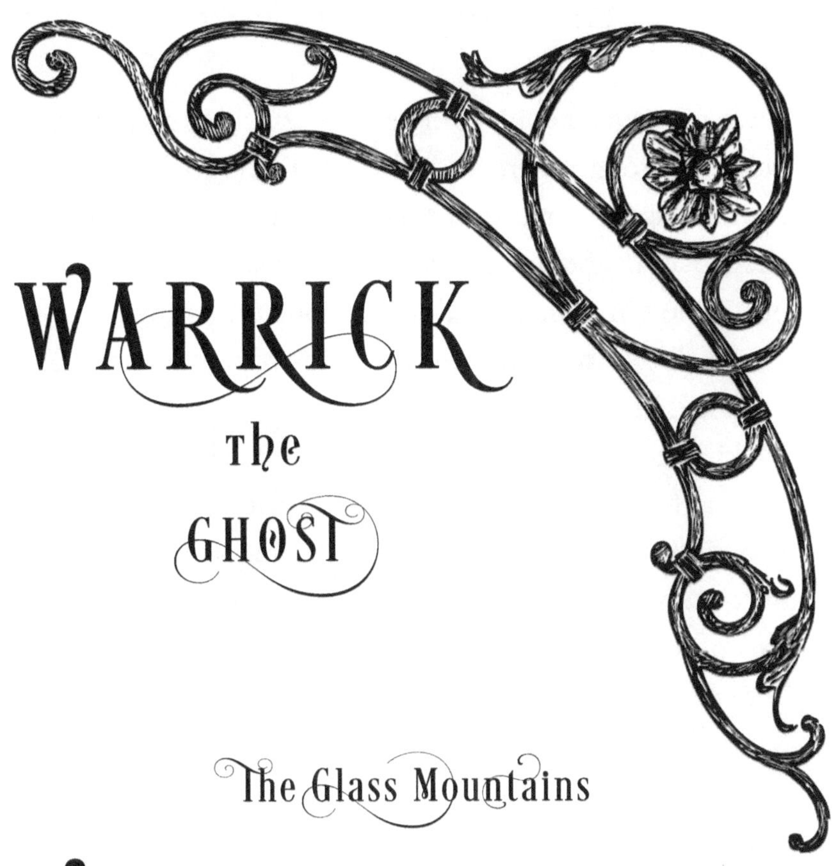

WARRICK
the
GHOST

The Glass Mountains

Warrick had thought seeing Elina suffer the purge was agony. He had known nothing.

Agony was seeing his Elina, and she was never laughing. Agony was seeing the dullness of her eyes and the numbness of her heart.

Agony was Elina never seeing *him*. Not as he rode beside her. Not his horse or any of his possessions.

Yet she whispered his name in her sleep. Every night, he lay beside her—and at times it seemed she knew he was there, though they could not touch. Yet he could breathe in her sweet scent. He could feel her breath, her warmth.

And he could help her. Protect her. Though Warrick

could not touch her horse or belongings without his fingers passing through them as if through air, he could perform some tasks for her as they traveled and made camp—and she'd had attendants for so long that she likely did not notice how much seemed to get done on its own.

Or she was too numb to notice. Too hurt to see anything.

Until her storm of rage and tears.

He knew not what had set her off but he was glad of it. Glad to see something other than that horrible *nothing*. Though it had been agony, too, watching as her fury and hurt erupted from so deep within that it seemed every part of her heart must have been shattered. Agony to see her stagger back and sink down in front of the fire, her face in her hands, her chest heaving with sobbing breaths.

Throat aching and thick, he knelt beside her. "I am here, Elina." He'd seen how often she looked down the road behind them, as if waiting for him to come. "I am here, and I wish for nothing more than to hold you. Tie the ribbon again. I cannot bear this."

He laid the ribbon before her, praying she would see it. The ribbon and the vows they'd spoken were not his or hers, but *theirs*.

When she spotted it, her breath caught on a gasping shudder. Her reddened eyes stared in wonder. Her brows drew together in confusion.

She glanced around as if searching for how it had come to be on the ground, her gaze sweeping through Warrick before returning to the ribbon. With a trembling hand, she reached for it.

More tears spilled down her cheeks as she slid the satin through her fingers, weaving through them as on the day of their wedding. Her thumbs smoothed over the severed ends, where the cut edges had begun to fray, though the rest of the ribbon had not.

"Tie it, Elina," he urged hoarsely. "I've hurt you, I know this. But I beg you to let me make it right."

Again she glanced up, her eyes searching the road—then squeezing shut again, her breath hitching brokenly. The ribbon crumpled between her fisted fingers.

"Foolish girl," she spat. "After all this. You still want to believe in that stupid prophecy, to pretend that there is any true magic within you. As if *you* could speak any wish into truth." Sobbing, she pressed her hand to her face, her tears soaking into the red satin. "As if your love has *ever* changed anything. As if anyone has *ever* loved you."

"I do. My wife, my queen." Desperately Warrick cradled her face in his hands, feeling her phantom warmth and the wetness of her tears as they dripped from her chin. "I love you. Please, Elina. Believe in what you've done. In what you can do. It *is* magic. True magic. Tie the ribbon, and you will see."

Slowly her sobs eased. Her despairing gaze turned to the road.

"I am here, Elina," he said thickly. "I am here."

She looked down. For the first time, he noticed the blood between her thighs. With the ribbon in her hand, she drew her fingertip through the crimson smear on her skin. New tears slipped down her cheeks before she took a deep, shuddering breath. Resolve hardened her silver eyes.

She flung the ribbon into the fire.

Heart ripping open, Warrick plunged his hand into the flames even as the ribbon flared bright and hot. The burning satin slipped through his fingers.

Then there was nothing of it left to save.

"Onward," Elina said wearily, and picked up her axe as she rose to her feet.

Warrick remained on his knees, staring at his blistered hand. In his palm were a few crumbles of ash. Never could she tie the ribbon again. Never could she remarry him, or see him or hear him. Always it would be this way—watching his wife, protecting her, but unable to touch her or speak to her. And Elina would forever believe she was unloved.

He had not known what agony was.

SHE CRIED HERSELF TO SLEEP that night. Warrick held her as best he could, his body enmeshed with hers where they touched, sharing his warmth. She stirred ever so slightly when he pressed a phantom kiss to her hair.

"Warrick," she sighed against his skin.

Asleep. Yet not completely. A few times before she'd seemed aware of him at the moment she hovered between sleep and dreams. Just as some people from the corner of their eye saw ghosts that disappeared when looked at straight on, Elina sometimes sensed him.

He swallowed past the ache in his throat, breathed past the devastation that had settled into a crushing weight upon his heart. "I am here. I love you, wife."

"Wished for a child," she mumbled into his chest. "To have you."

Then she'd bled. Understanding sliced through him, splitting open his chest. "You will always have me. Never will I leave you."

"It hurts so much." A sob hitched through her breath. "I think I might die."

"You are too strong for that." As she'd been during the purge. As Warrick must be, too. No matter the agony. The burning of the ribbon changed nothing. Always he would be her husband. Never would he want anything else. "Sleep now, my wife. All will be well."

"My husband." Sighing contentedly, she nestled deeper into him and murmured, "I love you."

Then all *would* be well. Mayhap Elina could not believe in the powerful magic that was her love.

But Warrick did.

THE GLYPH ON WARRICK'S CHEST began glowing brighter in the foothills of the Glass Mountains. And brighter.

Elina had once spoken to Serjeant Iarthil of these mountains being haunted, yet by her tone she'd believed the haunting was nothing but a tale told to frighten children. Had Warrick not been pretending he understood nothing of what she said, he would have told her what he'd already known.

The Glass Mountains were swarming with ghosts.

The first time he'd visited Galoth—the same journey that he'd been named the Trollslayer—Warrick had heard of the haunted mountains. He'd learned not to dismiss such tales, whether they were called blights or children's stories, or whatever name they were given to comfort those who would never rest easy knowing what resided in their midst.

So Warrick and Bannin had ridden north. Such a young fool he'd been then. After his pride had taken the beating of becoming the Trollslayer, Warrick had indulged in a vision of himself striding into the mountains and righting countless wrongs, then returning triumphant to Galoth and earning a name that wasn't a jest.

Upon seeing how *many* ghosts there were, however, he'd known something was different. Most never traveled beyond where they'd once lived or where they'd died; they haunted the spot where their bodies lay or where something important was hidden. And whether a wrong was righted or not, the death of the one who'd wronged them—or the death of the person they'd wronged—often marked the end of their haunt.

Yet the ghosts in the Glass Mountains had not lived or died here. Instead they'd been drawn to the mountains from every corner of the world. By what power, Warrick knew not. He'd only been able to talk to a few, as many spoke in ancient tongues that no one alive still used. Because in these mountains, death was not an end to their haunt. Every ghost that he'd spoken to had committed wrongs for which there was no hope of making right—the slavers and tyrants and invaders whose wrongs compounded generation after generation, long after those directly harmed were long gone.

Warrick could do nothing for these ghosts. He did not *want* to do anything for them. Let them wander aimlessly. Eternally. With all their ambitions of greed and power reduced to naught but a children's tale.

It would be a fine unresting place for Elina's uncle, as well.

Yet the living had no place here. Beyond the foothills, the mountains were more barren than the Dead Lands, with sharp and gleaming glass peaks and a road of crushed black stone that wound through obsidian canyons. Nothing grew. Rainwater formed crystalline pools and streams yet no green lined their banks. Even the constant buzzing of summer insects had fallen to an eerie silence.

Though Elina could not see the dead milling around them, she seemed to sense the strangeness of the haunt and hastened her mount along the road. Her unease deepened the farther they climbed toward the pass. She often twitched her head to the side, as if catching a glimpse of a ghost from the corner of her eye.

Then she laughed at herself, shook her head, and said aloud that what she'd seen was but the sun glinting on the glass—as if speaking those comforting words would make it true. Yet she must not have found much comfort in them, for she nudged her horse to an even faster pace.

Darkening clouds gathered overhead. Elina glanced at the sky, then ahead to where a knife-edged ridge marked the spine of the mountain range and the pass to the northern side.

"What do you think?" She patted her gelding's neck, as if reassuring the animal, yet Warrick suspected she merely sought a connection with any living thing in this place. "Can we reach the pass by nightfall? Even if not, a full moon rises tonight. We should be able to see clearly if those clouds disperse." Another look at the gray sky made her grimace. "Oh, but I wish to get through this place as quickly as we can. I would rather cross in two days than three…and I'd rather spend one night here than two."

The gelding tossed his head and nickered.

Elina nodded. "We will try, then."

Warrick grinned. One day, somehow, he would tease her about relying on her horse's judgement. Yet he could not fault her decision. Though he felt none of the unease that Elina did, he also had no wish to spend two nights in these mountains.

They continued on. Elina put up the hood of her traveling cloak as it began to rain, a dreary drizzle that seemed disinclined to empty out the clouds overhead.

The day faded. The gray sky offered no hints of red and orange to mark the coming of night. Darkness crept in, as if every shadow opened its maw and slowly swallowed the mountains, then the heavens.

Yet not *all* was dark.

The number of ghosts in proximity to Warrick made his archer glow fiercely, brighter than ever before. Bright enough to light their way.

The glyph had been shining since Galoth, yet not with such intensity. In the day, the glow touched nothing at all; at night, the hint of golden light it cast upon Elina's skin or any of her things was easily mistaken for firelight.

Now she looked about in utter confusion. She could not see Warrick or his glyph—the source of the glow—yet by the shadows it cast, clearly the light radiated from a spot alongside her. Her baffled gaze turned to the sky, as if to check whether the moon had peeked through the clouds or refracted off the glass mountain peaks to illuminate the canyon through which they traveled.

Abruptly she whipped her head to the side. Likely another ghost from the corner of her eye. Yet instead of nudging her gelding faster, she drew him to a halt and peered intently at the canyon wall.

In the dark, the sheer glass face acted as a warped and striated mirror, catching the light from his glyph…and the reflections of the ghosts near to the obsidian.

Warrick stared in astonishment. He'd *never* seen a ghost reflect before. Not on water, not near glass. Yet whether because of the magical nature of the light illuminating them or the haunted obsidian glass, their mirror images were visible as if they were trapped within the canyon walls.

Visible to Elina, too. She'd urged her horse closer to the obsidian cliff. Her gaze fixed on the ghost nearest to her, a delicate woman whose slitted throat was draped in emeralds.

She drew a shaky breath. "I see you." That tremulous announcement was followed by a lifting of her chin and a firmer, "Who has wronged you?"

Just as she had heard Warrick ask the murdered woman by the bridge. Elina meant to right this one's wrongs.

Never had he loved her more. Heart full, he drew Troll up alongside her. "That one is not worth the effort."

Elina gave a startled cry. She looked wildly about, pulling her reins this way and that, her gelding prancing anxiously in response to her agitated movements.

Searching for a threat, Warrick pivoted Troll around. Nothing but ghosts. Then his sluggish brain caught up to what her reaction meant.

She'd heard his voice. Mayhap only as an echo from the obsidian, but it mattered not why.

She'd heard him.

"Is someone there?! Who—" She froze, staring at the darkly mirrored wall. Her chin quivered. "Warrick?"

And now *saw* him. His reflection was a wavering, mounted figure in the glass, his glyph glowing as brightly as a bonfire.

Swallowing thickly past the joy clogging his throat, he managed a ragged, "I am here, Elina." Then a near giddy laugh broke from him. "As the lantern you once said I would be."

A choked, stuttering noise escaped her. In lurching movements, she swung her leg over the horse's back and dropped from the saddle, then stumbled to the obsidian cliff. She raised trembling fingers to touch the surface of his reflection, then spun to look behind her, her gaze searching frantically before returning to his image in the glass.

"Where?" Her voice broke on the word.

"Right behind you." His heart thundered as he dismounted. "Where I've been all this time, wife."

"But— No. *No!*" Grief crumpled her face. Her hand flew to her mouth and she bent over on a keening sob. "When? *How?*"

"I'm not dead!" In two strides Warrick was behind her, bracing his hands against the sheer obsidian, his body surrounding hers. This close, his reflection was clear and bright. "I'm not dead, Elina. I'm here. Feel me. Close your eyes, and feel me against you. Feel how I'm with you."

Stifling her sobs against her fist, she pressed her forehead to the canyon wall. Slowly she quieted, though tears still swam in her eyes when she lifted her head and saw him in the glass.

A shuddering laugh of a breath shook from her. "Warrick?"

He grinned. "Good eve to you, wife."

"But—" She twisted to look over her shoulder, then

back to the mirror. "How?"

"The priestess warned us."

Her brow furrowed. "She said nothing at all."

"Not Anhera's. The priestess who married us." Her warmth seeped into him as he pressed closer. "When the ribbon was cut, we became as if dead to each other."

"As if dead— Oh." Her shoulders bowed and she clasped her hand over her eyes, her body shaking, but Warrick knew not whether she was laughing or weeping. *Both*, he realized when she lifted her head. Her fingers pressed to the glass again. "Is that Troll?"

"He is here with me. We each have what is ours."

"I took your axe."

"I gave it to you."

Her lips folded in as if against another sob. "And you meant to take my head with it." Sniffling, she wiped her cheeks. "You were hardly the first with that intent. But I had wished…"

Tears spilled over and she buried her face in her hands. Everything within him ached to touch her. To hold her.

Throat constricted, he said hoarsely, "You wished to be loved."

She roughly swiped the tears away. "More fool I."

"You are no fool. You got what you wished for."

"When you laid eyes upon my face and your world overturned?" Her disbelieving scoff ripped at his heart. "I wanted so much to believe that stupid prophecy could become truth. To believe your heart was mine and that you'd always follow me. But when you looked upon me, you thought to kill me—and you only followed me for the jewels. Only took me to bed so that I would give them up. And to bring your friend my head."

Follow her? Was that part of the prophecy? He'd heard nothing of that bit, then. "I did not follow you from the prison, Elina. I was ahead of you and your retinue."

She bit her lip. "Perhaps. But you were not overturned when—"

"I did not lay eyes upon your face until the mudbeast. In the prison, all I saw was paint. The river washed it away."

Her breath caught, her silver eyes lifting to his. Still wary. But for the first time since Bannin had spilled the story of the golden hag, a gleam of hope shined from her face.

"I saw you under the water, Elina, and gave you my breath and my heart. And I have followed you here. I would follow you anywhere." His voice broke with emotion. "Can you still not believe? You *are* loved. More than anything."

She looked at him in wonder. "All this time, you were with me?"

"Every day when you looked back upon the road, I was there. Every night, I was at your side."

Realization dawned upon her face. "Telling me to tie the ribbon. To undo the spell. But I burned it." Horrified tears burst from her and she wildly shook her head as if to deny everything that destroying the ribbon meant. "Warrick, I burned it. I was so angry and hurt and I just—"

"I know, Elina," he soothed her, pressing a kiss to her head, letting her feel his warmth. "I was there. But the ribbon matters not. Love is the most powerful of all true magics. Ours will be strong enough. It will be powerful enough to overcome this spell."

"Stronger than the magic within the Stars of Anhera?"

"It will be. And we will find a way."

"I should have stayed to listen," she whispered, her voice filled with self-recrimination. "Then I would have known when you first laid eyes upon me."

"And I should have told you what I'd believed in the prison *before* Bannin shouted it from a table."

"Why did you not?"

She could not know how many times Warrick had asked that of himself. "Shame, to begin. Knowing how I'd wronged you with every word and thought. And I intended to tell you. When we might laugh over it."

A reluctant smile tugged at her lips. She lifted a shoulder in a half-shrug. "It *was* rather ridiculous."

"If it were not about us, yes? And if—" His jaw clenched as painful emotion piled up in his chest. When he continued, his voice had thickened. "To begin, it was only the shame of how mistaken I was. But as I came to know you, came to understand what you were to me... *Elina*, I would have let you drown. And I would never have known. Never have— I would have let you. You were *right there* and I would have..."

She touched her fingers to his tortured reflection. "But

you did *not*, Warrick."

"I came so near. I came so near to losing you. I can hardly bear to face what I intended." What he'd almost done—or *not* done, if he hadn't seen her face. "I would never have known. I would never have known that you were my heart and you would be…" Dead. The devastation of the mere thought choked away the rest. After a long moment he said, "Mayhap there will never come a day when I might laugh about it."

"One day, you will. I will make certain that you do."

His throat closed. *One day.* As if she meant to be a part of his days to come. "You have been betrayed so many times, Elina. I should have taken more care, and placed your fears above my own shame and regret."

"And I should have waited for you to explain your shame and regret—but never once did I imagine you might have reason to remain silent other than to trick me and then conceal the betrayal from me. Never did I consider what your feelings might be." Her gaze dropped to the ground. In a small voice, she added, "Since I have met you, I have come to see a selfishness in me that I cannot like."

"*Selfish*—? Have you lost your sense, woman?!" It bellowed from him and her gaze shot to his in astonishment. Good. Never did he wish to see Elina lower her eyes in that diminished way again. "You wished to be loved. That is no selfish wish. But beyond what you hoped to feel, what was your purpose? To kill your uncle. To help your people. And the moment—*the very moment*—I told you of Anhera's stars, you gave not a thought to your own life. Your only thought was of returning them, to end Galoth's suffering. *Selfish*," he spat out the word like the rubbish it was.

"But I loved you, Warrick. If I knew your character enough to love, I ought to have trusted in you."

"Why?" he asked bluntly. "Elina, when someone is struck over and over again by the people they love, can you blame them for flinching when someone else they love raises a fist? Even if that person's intention is only to…" His words trailed off as he wracked his brain. "I cannot think why else to raise a fist."

Eyes suddenly alight, she said, "Might you raise a fist to the sky to curse the heavens? Might you raise a fist to frighten a cow? Or might you—"

A cow? "Why would—"

"—raise a fist because, whenever you do, that thick muscle in your arm flexes in such a beguiling way?"

"In this beguiling way, wife?" Warrick stretched out his arms and alternated the flex so that she could watch the bounce of his biceps in the mirror.

Elina dissolved into laughter, and Warrick thought his heart might burst. He wrapped his arms around her, and though he held a phantom, he could *feel* the heat of her flesh, the thrum of her blood, the reverberation of her heart.

His voice was hoarse. "To hear you laugh again, Elina…"

There were no words to describe the feeling within

him. Yet likely she felt the same. Her laughter quieted on a shuddering breath and she closed her eyes, hugging herself around her chest, their hands and arms enmeshed.

After a long moment, she asked uncertainly, "So I did *not* build the fire each night?"

"You thought *you* did it?" Warrick began to shake with laughter. He'd assumed she hadn't given any thought to it at all, so accustomed to being helped by her attendants. "Would you not have remembered at least once?"

"I was heartbroken!" she cried, swatting at his forearm but only slapping her own. "I hardly recalled any of the road I traveled each day, so it made perfect sense that I would also not recall building my fires. Not attending to my own actions while I performed some routine task seemed quite in line with the depth of my despair."

Was heartbroken. *Was.*

Warrick had never been happier. "Building a fire has never been a routine task for you. You are spoiled, woman."

"I am not—" Suddenly she drew herself up, lifted her chin. "I am the Radiant Queen of Aleron. My concerns are more lofty than the gathering of twigs and the striking of sparks. That is why I have a king consort whose only role is to keep me safe and warm."

So she did. "*This* king consort would also kiss that laugh from your lips, wife. Then he would push you up against this mirror and fuck his seed into you."

"Ohhh. That would be…" She licked her lips and let out a shaky breath, her widened eyes meeting his in the glass. "So you *would* fuck a ghost."

This woman— "I love you," he said fiercely. "I love you. And I *would* take you, in whatever bizarre form you are."

"As I would you. As we *will*. Somehow."

"You begin to believe in your magic again?"

"I know not what I believe in. Was it a prophecy that I spoke into truth that brought us here? Was it magic that made you follow? Or was it merely every choice we made and everything we felt?"

"Merely?" He smiled against her hair. "There is no difference between what we do and feel, and the true magic that comes from it."

"No difference?" At the confirming shake of his head, she shrugged. "Then what I believe is that I will not allow any other outcome, except that we *will* be fully together again." She closed her eyes and reached back, the warmth of her hand cupping his face. "You cannot know much I love you, Warrick."

"I can," he said gruffly. "For I *do* know, if yours is anything near to how I love you."

"I will trust in that." Her eyes opened. "What now?"

"Onward." He lowered his head to press a phantom kiss to the side of her neck. "And even do you not see or hear me, when you feel this warmth, you will know I am there. You will know where I am touching you. Shall I tell you how to please yourself in our bed?"

"No. *You* will tell me in our bed."

Determination steeled Elina's voice. Abruptly she

pulled out of his embrace, gripping her axe. With a grunt, she swung it at the canyon wall. Razor-edged shards flew.

"Careful of your eyes, woman!" Helplessly he watched, unable to stop her as she swung the axe again and again. "What do you think to do?"

"I will *not* be without you again." She bent and carefully sifted through the broken shards before selecting one the size of her palm. She angled it toward Warrick. A relieved breath escaped her when his reflection appeared on its shining surface. "If the magic that allows me to see and hear you resides in the obsidian itself, then even outside of these mountains, I should still see and hear you…however small and faint you might be in a mirror of this size." She scraped its broken edge against a rougher piece of stone, dulling its sharpness—making the shard safer to carry and hold. "When Soren is dead and my kingdom freed, I will return to these mountains. And if I must, I will remove each peak to Aleron, so never will you be away from me."

His brilliant queen. "You would move mountains for me?"

"I would." Glancing up from the shard, she arched a brow at his reflection. "Add *that* to the legend that you will tell Bannin. Along with…what was it? Breaking curses with your cock?"

Warrick had no response to that, except to flex his arms at her again.

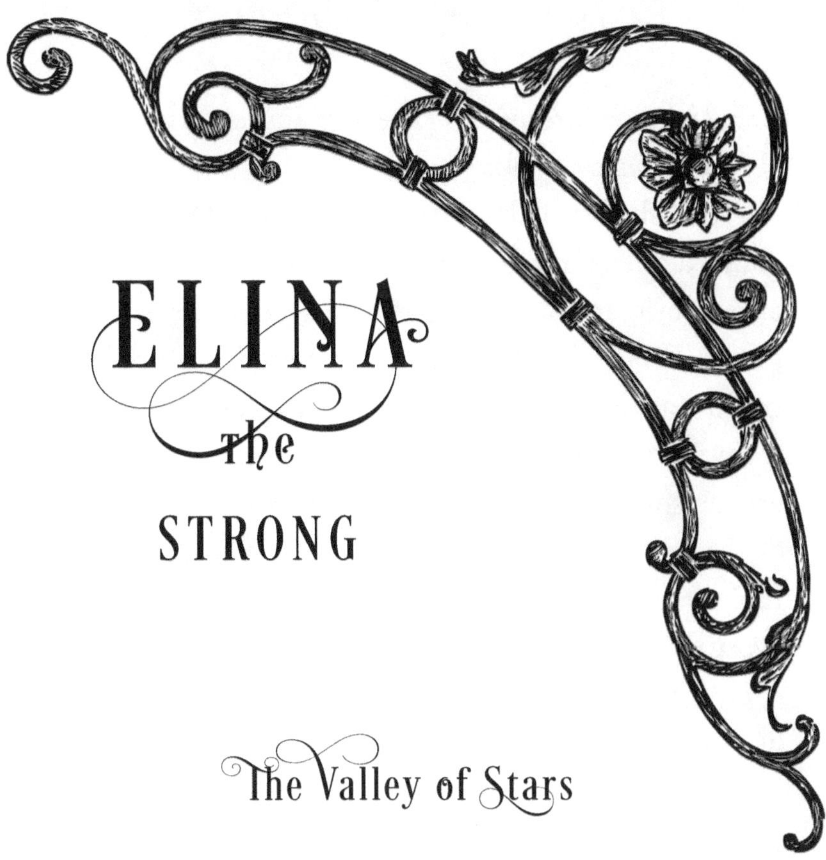

ELINA *the* STRONG

The Valley of Stars

"Aleron is just beyond this long canyon," Elina said and nudged her horse down a steep slope in the road which led to a narrow, stonebound passage that followed the winding of a river. "Though everyone in the surrounding kingdoms calls it a valley, because it widens farther north—the Valley of Stars. You will see why that name when night comes."

"Or you might tell me now, wife."

"It is more impressive to see."

"I have better things to look upon at night than a valley. Unless it is the valley between your thighs." When she laughed and shook her head, Warrick added, *"And the*

sound of your voice always pleases, so I would hear you speak of things that bring you joy."

Then she would be speaking mostly of Warrick. Elina glanced to the right, where she knew he rode, then down at the obsidian shard that she held against her leg with its glassy surface facing him. On a sunny day, his reflection could hardly be discerned and his voice sounded as if from a distance. Yet at night, lit by the soft glow of his archer, she could better see and hear him.

Unless it was a day such as this. She eyed the sky, rapidly darkening with the thunderclouds that gathered every afternoon toward the end of the season. So it was in Aleron, too. It was a rare day in late summer that passed without a thunderstorm.

In the past weeks, since leaving the Glass Mountains, she'd appreciated such summer storms. With the sun hidden behind clouds, Warrick's reflection was easier to see and his voice easier to hear.

But they had not been in the Valley of Stars then. "I will tell you on the way. Let us hurry. We will not wish to be still in the narrows when the storm breaks."

"It floods?"

She nodded and kicked her gelding into a canter, knowing Warrick would follow. The faster gait meant that she could not keep the shard aimed at him, yet he could still hear and see her.

Pointing to the waterline on the rocky canyon walls, she called out loudly enough to be heard over her mount's hooves, which would have been pointless had the noise not been muffled in the layers of silt left by the frequent floods. "There are gems within the stone! The floods wash them through into Aleron!—so many, they have almost no value! Just as the gold does not! Such an enormous vein runs beneath the kingdom, it became utterly useless as currency! But it makes us very wealthy in other realms and when trading."

She slowed to let her gelding pick his way through the debris of a flood-splintered tree. "The summer before Soren murdered my mother, we came here—my mother and I and her retinue. Not my uncle. She had little time for me but, now and again, she taught me lessons. So we came here, and in the moonlight, the gems glitter like stars. And I tell you, Warrick—I was raised in Aleron's palace, surrounded by beautiful things. The finest of silks, the loveliest of jewelry, the most exquisite of chambers. Yet they were all *nothing* compared to the stars that night." Unexpected emotion tightened her throat. "And she told me then why the gems were worth so little, but said that Aleron *could* stem the flow, so that they were more valuable and rare. We *could* prevent anyone from coming to the valley to collect their own. But the queens of Aleron never did, because the gems' true worth was their beauty here, and we believed it should be shared by everyone. And there *were* people who came. From Aleron, from Tagdon—every summer, all summer, just to see. The entire length of the valley was full of people who came to see the stars. But what do I see now, Warrick? Nobody. And if this is a sign of the changes Soren has made *here*, then I am terrified by how much damage my uncle has likely done in Aleron."

Warmth touched her cheek. She clasped his phantom hand to her face and sighed. "So we had best go and kill—"

Her horse shied to the right, nearly jolting her sideways out of the saddle. The shard dropped to the ground. Barely did Elina catch herself before joining it, clinging to the gelding's long mane. Heat swept through her sides—Warrick, instinctively trying to catch her.

"I'm all right," she panted, dragging herself upright. "What happened? Why did he—"

The clatter of stones pulled her gaze upward. Horror grabbed hold of her throat.

A demon. There was no other word for the creature uncoiling itself from its roost within a crevice in the canyon wall. Though vaguely human in shape, with arms and legs and heads in the expected places, its length from snouts to tail was three times Warrick's height. Covered in reptilian scales, with forked tongues slicking out from its lipless mouths, it ought to have given the impression of some giant deformed beast. Yet no beast ever possessed such cold intelligence in its gaze, and it was that look which made Elina's blood freeze.

Her gelding's frantic neigh shattered the icy horror that had locked her in place. Swiftly Elina reached for her axe. More than anything, she wished to take a moment to retrieve the shard, to see where Warrick was, yet she dared not take her eyes from the demon as it slithered down the cliff.

Warrick had his own weapon—another axe that he had purchased along the way. He would surely be fine. Just as she would be.

Gripping the end of the axe's chain in her fist, she wrapped the links twice around her wrist. The axe-head, she let drop to the ground. She'd practiced this. So many times.

And she *was* strong enough.

A drop of venom fell from the demon's tail sting to sizzle upon the ground. Sharp, curved claws tipped its long fingers and toes. A dual grin revealed serrated teeth.

Its heads told her where Warrick was, she abruptly realized. One peered at her, the other watched him—at an angle that meant he was close beside her. She had not wanted to swing her axe if he was near, but in truth…her blade would simply go through him without harm.

"—*behind me, Elina.*" His voice reached her, barely louder than the demon's hiss. Troll must be almost on top of the shard but she did not spare a glance to see. "*That loose skin on its sides. It will—*"

Jump, diving toward them with legs and arms outspread, claws gleaming.

With a full twist of her body, Elina swung the dangling axe. It whipped upward in an arc the length of the chain.

The blade bit deep into the demon's left head, knocking

it out of its dive and sending it spinning—and yanking Elina by her arm from the saddle.

Her startled scream was blown from her lungs when she hit the ground, stunned. Barely did she hear Warrick's snarled, *"You are mine, fiend!"* before the pain of the impact walloped her belly and chest. She gasped for air and lifted her head just as the straining pull on her arm went slack.

The demon was…gone. The chain around her wrist led to her axe, which lay in the silt, the blade stained with blue blood.

Wheezing, she got to her knees. Her gaze searched the cliffs. But where…?

Silt suddenly flew in a wide arc past her. Then there was Warrick, his warmth passing through her flesh—followed by a cold slithering that left her gagging and coughing.

But she understood now. He'd claimed the demon as his…and it had vanished, as did everything of Warrick's. Then their battle had carried them both *through* her.

Blue blood splashed the cliff wall.

She scrambled for the shard.

"Your Highness!" a familiar voice shouted.

Astonishment whipped her around. Serjeant Iarthil approached at a gallop, unslinging his crossbow from his back. His gaze was fixed beyond her—on the fight she could not see.

He lifted the weapon to his shoulder but did not fire. His brow furrowed. "Is it dead?"

Another squelch of blood painted the ground. *"It is*

now. Is this the only fiend my queen wishes for me to kill?"

She found the shard, brushed away the dirt from its mirrored face—taking that brief moment to consider. No question whether she would ask Warrick to kill the serjeant—she would not. Yet what *did* she wish to do?

Once, it had been never to see the serjeant again. Yet he'd come anyway. And though everything within her screamed not to acknowledge him, to simply walk away…well, had she not learned her lesson? Perhaps the serjeant had reasons for his actions that were not meant as a betrayal. She could at least listen. That did not mean she would trust him.

"What is this?" Serjeant Iarthil stood over the demon she could not see, nudging it with his foot.

"Most likely what my uncle has wrought." When the serjeant frowned, as if not understanding, Elina huffed out a breath. "Surely you recall passing through Scalewood as we journeyed to Kael the Conqueror's four kingdoms? There were demons such as this there." And she'd been utterly terrified—her entire retinue had been—as they'd traveled through the forest with only invisible wards to protect them from the monsters and demons inhabiting the woods. "The spellcasters in Ivermere flagrantly and frivolously used their corrupted magic, and the result was Scalewood. Now my uncle casts his spells flagrantly and frivolously. This valley might very well be *our* Scalewood now."

And would be another explanation for why no one

was here. She'd thought her uncle had begun to hoard the gems—which he might also be doing—but such demons would keep people away.

"It did not happen so quickly in Scalewood," the serjeant said.

"Mayhap it happened more quickly here because it already did there."

"We cannot know, can we? And it is not what concerns me now." Elina fixed a pointed stare at her man-at-arms. "I gave orders for you to lead the others back to Aleron. Yet I do not see them behind you. Why have you come?"

"My duty to you—"

"No!" she said sharply. "Your duty *to me* was to lead the others. Yet you are here. Why?"

His jaw clenched. "My vow—"

"Was made to another. Whom do you serve, Serjeant? My dead mother or your living queen?"

"My honor demands that I protect you," he said quietly.

"So you serve yourself, not me."

"My vow is not to serve you but to keep you safe." His gaze fell to her hand. "I had heard that you no longer wear the rings. Yet you are well. You *had* been poisoned, not cursed?"

"Did you not believe what I had written?"

"You might have been coerced to write it." His gaze flicked over her shoulder, where she could feel Warrick's warmth as he stood behind her. "So that he could persuade you to leave us and travel to Galoth."

"The realm of bandits and warlords." She smiled bitterly. "You lied to uphold your vow to keep me away from Aleron."

His brow furrowed. "Never did I make such a vow. Only to keep you safe."

"Lady Faraine—"

"Betrayed you. I would not, my queen. Your mother only wished us to wait until someone took it upon themselves to kill Soren, as she was certain would happen. Then you were to return to reclaim your throne."

A little laugh shook through her. So her mother had not believed her too weak to be queen. Just too weak to face her uncle.

"I did wish that I had not promised to wait until Soren was dead—especially when this one seemed to fulfill the prophecy." He gestured to Warrick. "But my vow was only not to allow you to return before that time. And in that way, I also kept you safe."

"Then why not send Warrick ahead with his axe? Why take the slow route and keep us from Galoth?" The answer hit her like the lightning flashing in the distance. "You *knew*. You *knew* what the jewels were. And if we traveled through Galoth, the Stars of Anhera would be recognized and returned."

"And you would die." The serjeant confirmed her guess with that reply.

She shook her head, disbelief clawing at her gut. That he would conceal *this*. "You should have told me. Should have told me that people were dying and I had a way to help them."

"At the cost of your life, my queen? That was a decision that should not be made. My vow meant I did not have to."

"It was not your choice to make!"

"I had no choice, my queen." A muscle worked in his jaw. "And no lasting harm was done. Everyone taken by the curse was returned."

"No lasting harm?" She stared at him. "No lasting harm in the terror of watching your own limbs turn to stone? No lasting harm in watching it happen to someone you love? And what of the ones who hacked away part of themselves trying to stop it—those limbs did not return. What of the years lost locked in stone? The years they lost with their loved ones, and the years their loved ones lived without them, believing them dead? You have grieved, Serjeant. You know the agony of living and believing you will never again hold the person you love the most. Yet there was no harm done?"

Lowering his eyes, the serjeant said nothing.

"Do you know who stole them?"

Serjeant Iarthil seemed relieved not to have to answer Elina. "Soren paid to have it done. Your mother learned of his intention and intercepted the rings."

Elina frowned. "Yet she did not return the jewels? She must have heard of the curse that fell over Galoth."

"She kept them as protection against Soren."

"Kept them," Elina echoed, her heart suddenly sick

and heavy. "Though she knew people were dying."

"*She* would have died. Do not judge her without knowing, Your Highness. She never spoke of an intent to keep them forever. Only until she knew what her brother was plotting."

Elina narrowed her eyes. "Do you truly believe that? You follow her in all things. If my mother had said *anything* of returning them as quickly as possible, regardless of the risk to her own life, would you not have also followed her in that and told me what my mother hoped to do? Instead *you* made the choice for me that she did for herself, because you believe it was the right choice for a queen to make."

He looked away. After a moment he said, "In the end, it mattered not. Soren poisoned her. We fled while she still wore them. I know not what happened to the jewels before they landed in your lap."

Poisoned her. Soren had known exactly how to get around the jewels' protection. All that had saved Elina was Chardryn's rampant pride, which would allow her to poison her queen but not in such quantities that the poisoning would be obvious and besmirch her family's name. "It must have been quite the dose."

"*Or Anhera was not so inclined to protect her.*"

"Perhaps." Only minutes before, she'd been remembering how wise and generous her mother had been. To learn this of her now…Elina could not dwell on it. Her mother was dead, and Elina would have the rest of her life to sort through her feelings. Yet the serjeant stood before her now. "For two years, you let those people suffer. Did you intend to wait until I was dead to return them?"

"I would have first used them to defeat Soren, so the throne could return to its rightful line."

"Would you have taken Warrick's axe as well?"

"I had not yet decided."

"Are you here to stop me from returning to Aleron?" As his vow still demanded.

He gave to her a pained look. "If this"—he indicated the demon—"is what Soren's magic creates, nowhere near Aleron is safe, my queen. My honor requires me to take you away from here."

"I am *not* your queen. I have *never* been your queen. My mother has always been, and by keeping your vow to her, you have wronged me. But you can right that wrong by letting me be. I will not forget the many times you have truly saved me." Voice cold and firm, she made her decree. "But henceforth, you are relieved of your duty, Serjeant Iarthil. If you wish to return to Aleron, you will receive your pension. But I will not see you again. I know you believe your honor demands you to hold to your vow, but what you call honor is not honor at all. There is no honor in letting the people of Galoth suffer. No honor in lying to me instead of confessing your conflict. Should I trust a man who lies to his queen and leads her astray? I will not. Never will I trust you at my side again."

Though tears swam in his eyes, the serjeant stood

straight and unyielding. "Your dismissal does not change my vow."

Elina clenched her teeth in exasperation. "Then come and speak to my mother, and perhaps she will release you from it. Her ghost is likely in Aleron. So you may accompany us there, despite your vow to keep me away until Soren is dead. Or you can attempt to keep me here, but you can only accomplish that by harming me when you force me to stay. Either way, you break your vow. So which will it be?"

"Do not harm her, or I will *kill you. For she is* my *queen."*

The serjeant looked again over her shoulder, and whatever he saw upon Warrick's face made him stumble back a step.

A rumble of thunder filled the silence that fell between them. Elina cast her gaze at the sky. Gray sheets of rain were falling in the distance. "Oh, we are fools!" Distracted by the demon and the serjeant, she'd utterly forgotten the oncoming storm. "We must ride! Go!"

Grasping the shard and her axe, she hauled herself into her saddle and kicked the gelding into a gallop. She bent low over the horse's neck, the wind whipping at her eyes as the first drops of rain began to splatter around them. Yet these drops mattered not at all. Only the sheets of rain dropping onto the hills behind them.

An ominous rumble sounded through the canyon. Not thunder, but continuous. And closing in.

Her frantic gaze swept the cliffs on either side of the

river, which was already spilling over its banks. Worse was coming. They could not remain on the canyon floor. They had to get above the flood.

"There!" she shouted, pointing farther down the canyon. A narrow ledge of packed dirt that climbed the side of the cliff, with a path already worn upon its surface. Hardly more than a game trail, but it would take them up.

A monster surged out of the river ahead. Insectile. *Huge.* At a gallop Elina had barely a glimpse of it before she swerved her mount away from the overflowing banks and prayed the creature would not be fast enough to close the distance before they passed.

It skittered toward them like lightning.

"I have it!" Serjeant Iarthil shouted. "Get her onto the ledge! Go!"

The serjeant raced toward the monster. She had only a moment to see his crossbow bolt impale its dripping carapace and him leaping from his mount, blade in hand, before her horse carried her past.

She reached the trail—and oh gods, it was hardly worth the name. So narrow, with uncertain footing and disintegrating edges held in place by frail roots. They would all have a better chance on foot than riding. Quickly she dismounted, slapping her gelding's rump to send him ahead. She went next, hurrying as quickly as she dared—feeling Warrick's warmth that told her he was there.

The sprinkle of rain became a deluge. The soil at her feet began to tremble. She risked a glance back and her heart stopped.

The serjeant. Caught in the demon's pincers. With a wall of water behind them.

"Iarthil!" she screamed as the surging water slammed into them both.

Man and monster disappeared.

"Elina! Go!"

The ground shook. The flood roared past them—they were high enough, but the packed dirt that formed the base of the ledge was crumbling, the surface soil shivering as rocks and clumps of grass tumbled into the water below.

Elina scrambled faster, using her hands where the trail was steep and slippery with mud, crying out each time her footing gave way. She felt Warrick's warmth again and again, as if he kept trying to steady her—then the ledge abruptly collapsed under her feet. She screamed and lunged forward, the shard tumbling out of her grip and into the flood. The trail ahead was still firm, more rock than dirt. Her gelding trotted along without a care while Elina wildly snatched at bushes to anchor her weight and pulled herself onto a solid part of the ledge.

Warrick's warmth was gone. So was every bit of the trail behind her.

Terror razed her heart. She whirled around. *"Warrick!"*

Her scream echoed over the roar of the flood and the pounding rain. Desperately she searched the water below. If he'd fallen in, she could throw him the axe and pull him in by the chain. She was strong enough. But she could not *see* him. She could only see what was hers.

But Warrick *was* hers.

"You cannot take him from me!" she shouted at the river, at the rain, at the heavens. "He's mine! Mine! My husband, my heart, my life! Everything he is is mine! Everything I am is his! He is mine!"

A soft nicker from the trail just ahead. Troll.

She could see Troll.

But Warrick was where? Where? The water raced past, carrying trees and rocks but no barbarian.

"*WARRICK!*" she screamed, praying he would hear her. "Stay alive! Swim! I will pull you in!"

"Elina."

She whipped around—and there he was. Above the yawning gulf of the collapsed ledge, clinging to the rock face of the cliff, his every beautiful muscle taut with strain and gleaming with rainwater…and he was grinning.

Her breath whooshed out of her lungs and she collapsed to the trail. "If you think I will throw you my chain after you scared me in that way, you are sadly—"

With a great leap, he sailed over the gap and landed in a crouch at her feet.

"Elina," he said hoarsely.

Then she was in his arms, kissing him. "I love you," she said fiercely before taking his mouth again.

He growled against her lips. His hands gripped her ass. Her back hit the cliff wall. Then she was helping him, uncovering slippery and wet skin, and though Elina was not yet slippery and wet enough, she could not wait any longer than he. Her legs wrapped around his hips. Warrick grunted into their kiss as he tried to get in, then her flesh yielded and his thick shaft stretched her deeper and wider with every hard thrust.

Then this wild fucking was not just about joining with him, desperately taking him again, but so *good*. She broke for a breath and Warrick took it as he filled her again, each kiss starting and ending with a promise.

"Never again—"

"Always will I—"

"With you—"

"My heart—"

"Yours."

"Forever after."

Not a full vow was completed between kisses but Elina did not need all of the words. He pushed deep and her ecstasy burst, drenching his cock with her own sultry rain. Warrick groaned and quaked against her—then slowed, still rocking into her as she clung to his shoulders, her body limp and quivering.

"Every last drop," she whispered.

He barked out a laugh and buried his face in her neck. "It has built up, so there is much to wring out." His arms squeezed her tighter. "You found the way."

"In the end, it was rather simple. Wasn't it?"

"Simple would be vows that are not meant to be undone." He lifted his head to rest his brow against hers.

"And I suspect that merely saying 'you are mine' before would not have had such an effect. Your love *is* quite powerful, Elina."

"As is yours." Her fingers caressed his jaw. "The demon vanished when you claimed it as yours."

"I'd hoped it would."

"You thought it might?"

"I hoped. If it could not touch you, it could not harm you."

She curled her lip in irritation. "You didn't need to do that. Did you see what I did to it with the axe?"

"I saw. You killed that first head." He kissed the snarl from her mouth. "But I am your king consort. I keep you safe and warm."

"Oh. Very well, then." She felt his fingers slide up over her hip—then pause. His brow furrowed. "What is it?"

Slipping out of her, Warrick set her down and lifted the hem of her tunic, which they hadn't bothered to discard along with her riding trousers. "You have a ward," he said wonderingly.

She twisted to look. There, on her hip—a small glowing rune, just like the small rune that bound Warrick's innate magic to his skin. She pulled back to look at his chest. His archer was no longer glowing.

"We are no longer as if dead to each other, at least." Her fingers traced the shape his glyph made, then she exclaimed when Warrick suddenly released her hem and pulled down her neckline instead.

"No archer."

She frowned up at him. "Did you expect one?"

"After seeing the rune?" He nodded. "You have powerful magic, Elina. 'Everything I am is his. Everything he is is mine.'" With a fingertip, he followed the bare curve of her breast. "I did not always have my archer."

"What did you have?"

"Nothing. All of my skin would shine when I was in a haunt—yet not so brightly that it could be easily seen during the day. The glyph focuses that light, draws it into the archer's shape, so it is more noticeable. If we *do* share all that I am now, then having no archer might simply mean you should choose your own glyph. The archer is a mark that my family uses; that is the only reason I chose it."

"And I will see ghosts, too?"

"I cannot say. But this"—he tapped her hip—"will protect you against spells."

"Will it protect me from my uncle's spells?"

"'Everything he is is mine.' If my magic is stronger than his, this ward will be stronger than his spells," he said, his eyes gleaming. "But know this, Elina—his magic surely cannot be stronger than yours."

"Well, then." She grinned and kissed him, then hefted her axe. "Let us go kill my uncle."

WARRICK

the

RADIANT

Aleron

WARRICK WISHED THAT HE HAD NOT BEEN PROVED right so quickly. Elina *had* taken on his ability to see ghosts—and her kingdom was teeming with them. So many. Only in the Glass Mountains had he ever seen more, yet those were spread out over the expanse of the mountain range. In Aleron, they'd all gathered outside the city gates.

As if waiting for their queen to come.

With so many ghosts in one place, Warrick's glow had escaped the confines of the archer to spread over his skin. And Elina…

She truly was the radiant queen.

Every inch of her shone with golden light. No need for paint. *This* queen's face was no mask and an utter beauty to behold.

Except for her eyes. Those eyes were terrible to behold. They would have made even Warrick hesitate, had she ever made an enemy of him.

He'd thought she might be stricken with guilt and weeping, as she had been in Galoth. But as she looked upon the dead, he only saw her rage. Mayhap the guilt would come, undeserved though it was. But not yet.

At the gates, the guards let them through after a single glance, bowing to Elina with wonder and joy overspreading their faces.

The guards joined the crowd of the dead moving through the streets. As did many more of the living. At every turn, cries rang out about the Radiant Queen's return. A squadron of knights rode to meet them, swords and lances at ready—no doubt sent by Soren or in response to a suspected invasion. Elina needed no crown for them to recognize her as their queen. She merely looked to them with her terrible eyes and ordered them to fall in behind.

They did.

Why the guards and knights had not already killed her uncle was something Warrick would find out answers to later. For now his only concern was Soren, and the more warriors at her side, the better.

"What has put that look upon your face, my radiant king?" Elina had turned her gaze to him—her silver eyes not so terrible now with her teasing.

He could not smile. "If I had but sent a message, Bannin would have come with more warriors from Galoth. You would have more swords at your side."

"We have enough." She looked ahead. "And Galoth owes me nothing."

"It was not you who took Anhera's stars."

"It was Aleron…and I *am* Aleron. That I returned the jewels was merely righting a wrong done by mine own. And it is not fully made right, Warrick. You know it can never be." She glanced at him and smiled. "Best that we do it this way, with the people of Aleron behind me, reclaiming their kingdom."

With the queen reclaiming her kingdom. Elina rode into the palace courtyard and dismounted, carrying her axe. Warrick had his own—considering the prophecy, he could not have too many.

She strode forward with a shield on her arm. Spells cast at either of them would not likely harm them, but it would not save them from what the spells did to objects around them. Even with the wards, they could still be drowned. Or stabbed by a blade tossed by a whirlwind.

"Uncle!" Elina shouted, turning a slow circle in the center of the courtyard, her radiant glow almost painful in its intensity. "I am too old now to play hide-and-find! Show yourself, Usurper!"

"I had heard you were cursed, little niece of mine." Soren's voice echoed from all around them, making it impossible to pinpoint his location. Warrick's gaze searched the shadows for the man that Elina had described. "It is a rather lovely curse, if that is why you shine so radiantly."

"It is a gift!" she called out. "To right wrongs."

"Wrongs?" His laugh rang out from everywhere and was answered by the rattle of the knights' armor, as they all looked about uneasily. "I already righted many wrongs. Your mother was weak. And your father?"—a sound of disgust was followed by a spitting noise—"Then there is you, cursed and ill. You have been dying for *years*, Elina. Should you not admit how frail and weak you are? Do not the people of Aleron deserve a strong ruler?"

Elina scoffed. "I had this same conversation with my nurse not so long ago. Cruelty is not strength."

Again he laughed. "You are still a little girl. Cruelty is necessary to maintain power." The voice came from one direction now—the north side of the courtyard. Both Warrick and Elina turned to face him. "Yet we will not call what I am about to do to you cruelty. We will call it…mercy."

Elina's description would not have helped Warrick find her uncle, after all. Yet the man who emerged onto the steps of the palace in resplendent golden robes, an ornate crown, and a painted face could not have been anyone else.

Her amused laughter pealed through the courtyard. "Do you wear that every day, uncle? Or did you rush to put on a king's face when you heard I had come?" She made a sad little moue with her lips. "I know that costume is a terrible weight to bear. But fear not, I will take that heavy burden from your head and shoulders."

"Likely at the same moment that she takes the burden of your head from your shoulders," Warrick added dryly.

"Quite." Her mocking little pout dropped away, replaced by steel. "Surrender, traitor to the crown, usurper of the throne, murderer of your sister, the queen. With your cruelty and greed, you have betrayed every citizen of Aleron. And you *will* answer for it."

Soren came down a step, his eyes narrowed upon Warrick. "A warrior of the Dead Lands? You are no doubt warded against spells. Well, then."

His fingers flicked. With a shout, Warrick spun back to back with Elina, braced against the rapid thunk*thunk*thunk of arrow after arrow striking their tall shields, as her uncle used his magic to shoot quiverful after quiverful at them.

Soren's laughter echoed around them when the assault stopped. "Do you think I know nothing of your false prophecy, Elina? Of how your axes are meant to kill me?"

Grunting, he jerked his hands back. Warrick jolted forward as his weapon tried to rip away from his grip. Beside him, Elina cried out. She'd lost all but the chain that she'd wrapped around her wrist. The axe-head hovered above the ground at the end of the straining length, as if captured mid-flight as it was escaping her.

Yet now she was being pulled with it, as if she was being dragged by an ox.

Or something stronger.

Warrick let go of his axe. It shot out of his grip and flew up the stairs past Soren with enough force to shatter the steel blades against the palace's marble wall.

Warrick rushed to Elina, even as Soren grunted again and pulled harder. "Let go! It's hurting you!"

"I can hold it!" Agony sharpened her voice to the edge of sobbing. "I'm strong enough."

"You're strong enough to let go," he said urgently, wrapping his arms around her and gripping the taut length of chain, trying to ease the crushing pressure around her wrist. "*You* spoke the prophecy into truth with your kindness and your love and your hope for your people. Your magic *is* strong enough to make this axe fell a tyrant. Now believe in it, Elina. And let go!"

With a scream, she released the chain and stumbled back against Warrick's chest. His arms wrapped her tight.

The axe flew harmlessly past Soren.

The smirk had just formed upon his lips when, with a snap like a great dragon's tail, the chain whipped around his neck.

With a strangled cry, he was jerked off his feet. Warrick was already moving, charging up the stairs toward the sorcerer, who was clawing at the chain too desperately to flick his fingers with another spell.

Dagger in hand, Warrick slammed his knee into Soren's back, holding him down as he cut through the heavy silk of his robes—then flesh. With angry slashes, he marked a rune into Soren's skin.

The same rune that Warrick had. A ward against spells…but also one that locked his spellcasting magic beneath his skin. This sorcerer would be tossing no more arrows and axes around.

Soren screamed for mercy and for Warrick not to kill him. A coward at the end.

"You are not dead," Warrick snarled at him. "Not yet."

Gripping his powdered hair, Warrick hauled him up. Cradling her injured wrist, glowing brilliantly, Elina slowly glided up the stairs, regarding her uncle with her terrible, rage-filled eyes.

"Have you anything you wish to say to him first?"

"No," she said coldly. "But show him what he has done. Let him see."

Gladly. Warrick dragged the crying man forward to the edge of the steps, then touched him skin to skin. Soren sucked in a horrified breath. Silent. Staring out at the multitude of ghosts crowding the large courtyard, the sheer number of people he'd wronged.

"When you reach your journey's final end, all of them will be waiting for you."

Soren began to whimper and plead. Warrick ignored him.

Elina came to his side, looking out at the crowd of ghosts. Looking at *one* ghost, Warrick realized. A woman in a crown and gold raiments, and wearing the queen's face.

"Do you wish for me wait so that you might speak to

your mother?"

"And what would I ask? Why did she think me too weak to face my uncle? Why did she condemn a kingdom to the stone sickness when she might have ended their curse? What do those reasons matter now? Those wrongs are righted—as much as they can be—and all that remains is the harm they've left behind." Elina closed eyes that were glimmering with tears. "I have nothing to say to her."

Then only one thing needed to be done. Standing before the citizens of Aleron, living and dead, Warrick snapped Soren's neck.

Cheers erupted from the living. Elina's mother vanished, along with most of the other ghosts. Yet not all. With her radiance fading to a soft glow, Elina looked to the dozens upon dozens left.

"We still have so many wrongs to right. There must have been many here who followed my uncle's lead. Even a sorcerer cannot rule without support."

Warrick nodded. "You see to the living. I will see to the dead. We will sort out your kingdom."

"And yours." Elina smiled and took his hand, stepping over her uncle's body as she led Warrick down the stairs toward her celebrating people. "Will you stay by my side, my king?"

"I would be at your side in all things. And behind you."

Laughter danced in her eyes. "Like a pig?"

He gave a shout of laughter and swept her up into a kiss. The cheers from the courtyard became a roar of approval, but hardly did he hear them as Elina wrapped her arms around his neck and returned his kiss with all the love she had within her. She drew back, and Warrick looked upon the face of his wife, his queen—the woman he would gladly follow until the end of eternity.

"Elina," he said. Then kissed her again.

ELINA the LOVED

EPILOGUE

Three Years Later

"WARRICK," ELINA WHISPERED AS SHE SLID INTO THEIR bed. "Are you awake?"

"I am not," her husband mumbled. "Have pity on me, woman. I have spent these past three days hunting a demon in the valley."

"I know well where you have been, my radiant king. And it was not inside me, where you ought to be." Beneath their furs, her hand found his shaft already stiffened. "Ohhhh. I would say that you are *quite* awake. The only pity I will have for you is that your cock is so hard while you yet asleep. So I will use it for my pleasure alone."

"Then use it, wife." His eyes remained closed. "For even

as I sleep, my cock will always be at the queen's pleasure."

Grinning, Elina straddled him, loving how his breath shuddered when she encased his thick length within her silken warmth, well-primed by these days of waiting and the anticipation of his return to their bed. She braced her hands upon his chest and began to rock her hips, wishing she could kiss him—yet it was not so easy with her belly in the way.

She settled for teasing him. "Your poor cock. Your queen's pleasure has been insatiable these past months, has it not?"

He slitted open an eye. "I have noted no difference."

She chortled out a laugh and Warrick suddenly angled up to sitting, catching her mouth in a kiss. "I love you, my wife." One of his big hands gripped her ass, helping her ride him while the other went to her clit.

At the first stroke of his thumb over that sensitive bud, her laughter strangled into a cry against his mouth. "Warrick!"

"I have you." Rolling them onto their sides, he hitched her thigh over his hip and slid into her again, again. "And you have me, Elina. Taking me into your tight little cunt. Three days without laying my eyes upon your face, woman—it is an agony I wish to never feel again. Do you feel how deeply I love you?"

So deep. She caught his mouth in a gasping, panting kiss. His fingers returned to her clit, rubbing in rhythm with the slick plunge of his rigid flesh. Her body began to shake and he increased his pace, lifting the leg over his hip higher to thrust harder, faster.

She came apart when he was deep inside, her swollen inner walls clutching as she cried and writhed against him. Warrick gripped her thigh and held her open for his final grunting rut, then shoved his length full deep as his cock throbbed in release.

Elina held him close, smiling against his throat as his hips rocked again, though they were both soft and slick. "That last drop cannot do much now."

"Even when you are with child, I still wish to fill you with my seed." Warrick rolled onto his back, carrying her with him to straddle his hips. "I like to look at your cunt as it overflows with my spend and know you have taken all of me."

"Bizarre," she murmured, even as her sheath clenched around his softened flesh in response.

Warrick shook with quiet laughter, and she crawled up his body to nestle in at his side. He pressed a kiss to her hair. "Have you had your breakfast?"

"I have," said she, smiling. "I was at the table when I heard you return."

"Has your father gone?"

"I tossed him out within an hour of his arriving. His daughter, though—she has stayed. My sister." Elina was still unused to calling the girl such. "She says that she wishes to learn how to be a queen. I asked Dara to attend to her. I trust she will let me know if there is anything I *should* know."

He stiffened. "You suspect treachery?"

"I suspect that my sister despises our father and will use any excuse to escape his palace. I think it is no more than that…but I do not trust her yet, though she is hardly more than a child." She sighed. "Should I?"

"No," he said bluntly. "Trust is earned. It will likely take her some time to trust you, too." His strong arms gathered her closer, his hand curving over her belly. "And you are well?"

"I am." She entwined her fingers with his. "That sickness at the beginning truly was nothing." And Warrick had worried every moment. The warrior who'd stoically held her through the purge had been a near wreck every time she'd lost a bit of her breakfast. "All will be well," she added before his thoughts could turn to the labor that would soon come.

"Then I will believe it." He brought their entwined hands to his mouth, kissing her fingers. "What other news?"

"I received a missive from Queen Anja of Grimhold. They are inviting hunters from all kingdoms to come and be trained—especially from kingdoms such as ours, where the magical scaling has erupted beyond control." Which was why Warrick had been gone these past days. No matter how many demons and monsters they slayed in the Valley of Stars, more appeared—though her uncle was dead and they'd restricted spellcasting within Aleron to healing critical injuries. "She believes that the increase in scalemonsters is the sign of another Reckoning to come."

The last Reckoning, generations and generations past, had almost destroyed the realms that became the Dead Lands—and all the people living there.

Warrick's body had tensed. "Where?"

"Who can say? But Anja wishes to be prepared. As do I."

"So we will be." He rubbed her belly. "This one might be a huntress, then?"

"She will be whatever she wishes to be—and will have to find *something* to occupy her time. It will be many years before I die and relinquish the throne."

"Many, many years," Warrick said seriously.

Smiling, she tipped her face up for his kiss, then laid her head on his shoulder. Her palm smoothed over his chest and came to rest over his heart.

His archer was no longer glowing—just as Elina's skin was not. It had taken some time to root out all of those who'd taken advantage of her uncle's cruelty to do their own. But it was not only the dead who'd been wronged, and Elina had spent the past three years trying to right the wrongs done to the living citizens of Aleron.

"My father will likely not appreciate the kind of queen that I teach my sister to be," she mused.

"The kind of queen you are will see him for the indolent king that he is and remove him from the throne."

"I will not be sorry if she does." Nor would anyone in Tagdon, most likely. Elina tried to imagine that day—years in the future—when her sister would return home to claim her throne. She knew not yet whether to look forward to her leaving or to dread it. "Do you miss your family?"

"I do, but they are always with me. I know they are well. As they know I am."

She lifted her head. "How do you mean?"

"It is…a knowing. Between those in my family who share close blood." He caressed the swell of her stomach. "I will know of this one, no matter how distant she is. I know she is well now, that she is warm and safe. It is only you I worry about."

"Oh." She considered that. "I am glad she is well."

"I wish I knew of you, too."

"I don't. If we were closely related by blood we would not be making children at all. Or should not be. Do they in the Dead Lands?"

He laughed against her. "We do not."

"Well, then." She came up onto her elbow. "Send to them a message."

"My family?" At her nod, Warrick kissed her. "Perhaps they will come. Perhaps they will not. We might also one day go."

Which would be a journey of several years. Though intrigued by the thought, she said uncertainly, "We would have to deeply trust whoever we appointed to oversee Aleron."

"You *will* trust again. Your sister. Or another, like Dara."

"I hope so. Oh! Speaking of who might not be trusted… Lady Faraine has asked me if she can come home to

Aleron. I believe she envisions herself as a grandmother to our children. Or perhaps giving lessons to civilize my barbarian."

Warrick grunted. "What reply did you send?"

She gave a little shrug. "That she can return to Aleron if she wishes, but cannot expect to be given notice by me or anyone else within my royal court. I also mentioned my jealous barbarian king who seethes when he thinks of how she almost bound me unwillingly to a worthless prince."

And who was seething now at the reminder. His jaw clenched before he said, "You are kind to those who harm you."

"I do not think *they* will call me kind. The punishment for Nanny Char was exile and shame. The punishment for Lady Faraine will be denying her the importance that she desperately wishes to have in my life—and denying her anything that resembles control over me. But she *did* bring us together, in a fashion, because she knew I was searching for a warrior just like you." Her hair fell forward over her shoulder as she grinned down at him. "And something spiteful within me wants her to know that even though she used my hopes and wishes to concoct that false prophecy...it all came true."

"You made it come true."

"*We* did."

So often he spoke of how powerful her love and kindness was; yet never did Warrick seem to recognize how his love and kindness had overturned the world for her, too. How his care and support had saved her over and over. If only more people in her life had been even a bit more like Warrick.

But they had not been. "So I will let Lady Faraine see for herself the queen she called weak. Let her regret all that she did. Both she and Serjeant Iarthil possessed such a senseless kind of honor—only caring that they fulfilled their vows to my mother, regardless of my own wishes and will."

He cupped her face in his warm palm. "But his betrayal was more difficult for you. As was his death."

Though it had not truly hit her that he was gone until after her retinue had returned to Aleron. Then she had struggled and grieved. "He died as he would have wished to—while honoring his vow and keeping me safe. And… he truly *did* keep me safe for so long. Do you recall the mudbeast—"

He gave to her a grim look. "Never will I forget."

And still had not laughed at how near he'd been to letting a golden hag drown. "No, you would not forget," she said softly. "But you likely do not know that when I was pulled down, it was the sergeant who saved me before you did. He'd drilled into my mind how to defend myself. That kept me alive until you came. So I had much to thank him for. But then…I recall that he knowingly allowed the curse to continue for years. Which must be a wrong that outweighs all other rights. I know this."

"Yet your heart is still conflicted over how to remember

him. Your mother, too."

Elina had begun to think she would *never* know how to feel about her mother. "Yes," she whispered.

With tender fingers, he tucked a curl behind her ear. "A heart big enough to hold many feelings is a fine thing—though not an easy thing. But what is easy is not what makes us strong. And you have the strongest heart I know, Elina."

"It has not always been easy between us." She bit her lip, recalling the worst of those days. "After I burned the ribbon…have you ever wondered whether we should speak our vows again to remarry?"

"Not once. We *are* married. The vows and the magic that binds us need no ribbon. You are mine and I am yours—and if you ever said otherwise, and fully meant it, I believe that I would vanish again from your sight."

"You need not fear that." Her voice thickened and she felt the sting of tears that she tried to blink away. "Not having you with me would truly be a living death. One I have no wish to *ever* experience again."

Remembered anguish darkened his gaze. "I will always be sorry for hurting you as I did."

"I am not sorry. I learned much about myself in those painful days."

"Your supposed selfishness?" Warrick scoffed and levered up, pushing Elina over onto her back. "And what have you learned about yourself since, woman?"

A melting warmth stole through her flesh. "That I

am insatiable."

"So you are." His gaze hot, Warrick bent his head to her breasts, suckling her nipples and teasing until she was twisting helplessly beneath him—then he looked up at her expectantly. "And? What else are you?"

Breathlessly she said, "Yours, Warrick."

That answer pleased him, for he kissed his way downward—before stopping. "And?"

"Loved." She laughed from sheer happiness. "I am loved."

"So very much, Elina," he murmured against her skin. "You believe it?"

Heart full, her eyes swimming, she nodded. "I do."

Warrick pressed his lips to her lower belly, then peered up at her over the swell of it. "Shall I continue, my queen? I am hungry this morn."

So was she. Slipping apart her thighs, she offered up to her barbarian his favorite destination. "Onward, my king."

ERE WE ARE AGAIN, AT THE COMPLETION OF A SPELL—FOR that is all a tale is, words woven together in the hopes of making magic. A happily-ever-after lies ahead for our bride and her barbarian, and though that happiness does not always come easily, what is not easy only makes them stronger. More journeys they will take, more demons they will slay, more love they will make. And there will be more wrongs that need to be righted…for there is a Reckoning to come.

But that is a story for anotherwhere and anotherwhen— and this Midsummer's tale has come to an end.

• END •

Author's Note

If you are reading this in the days after waiting through the horrible fiasco of this book's initial release, thank you for hanging in there! Also, to everyone who sent a message to me via email or social media — I will try to respond to you personally in the upcoming days, but let me say here that your patience and support meant everything. It was truly kindness-as-magic in action.

Perhaps one good thing about that mess was that, in my rush to upload the book before the deadline, I didn't get a chance to write an author's note saying a few words about the book and what is coming next. So that's another error corrected.

And I am so thrilled I finally got a chance to write Elina and Warrick's story! It's been living in my head for almost six years (!) now, and all because of a slightly throwaway line in **The Midwinter Bride**'s epilogue. I added that to open the way to another story, because I had enjoyed writing that book so much, but I hadn't yet decided what the next one would be. But not much later, I pictured the scene where Elina the Widow is traveling alone through the haunted mountains with her unseen warrior following, and the rest of the story unfolded from that. I've been planning it for so long that details from this planned story ended up informing bits of the shorter stories, such as in **The Midnight Bride** when Mara tells Strax, "You understand, warrior, that I am from Aremond. I am not from a kingdom such as Savadon or Galoth, where they marry on a whim and untie their wedding ribbon when marriage no longer suits them. You'll always be bound to me." I always knew I'd be telling *this* story, so I tried to lay a bit of foundation for it in others.

And it took a while, but now that book is in your hands — and I hope you loved Elina & Warrick's romance as much as I do.

What's next?

I have another short story coming up for the Read Me Romance podcast, which will very likely be another Dead Lands story related to **The Stoneheart Bride**. That should be out in autumn of 2023. I also plan to write a little holiday suspense romance, where two enemies are stranded together in a cabin with **Only One Bed** — and at the same time trying to survive the assassins sent to kill them, because nothing says "this book is full of Christmas joy" quite like finding a dead body outside in the snow.

And then, a new fantasy series that's a spinoff of the Dead Lands called the **Daughters of the Hunt**. I hinted a bit at this in the epilogue, but if you want to know just a tiny bit more, you can always visit the page at my site. No pre-orders for it as of August 2023 (I won't be setting up pre-orders anymore until a book is finished and ready to be edited) but I hope to have **The Beast** done by the end of this year/beginning of next year. If you wish to be notified when it is released, please sign up for my newsletter! **I will never spam you or give away your information; it's only for book announcements.**

Until next time,
Kati

KATI ONLINE

Website: katiwilde.com
Email: kati@katiwilde.com
Newsletter: katiwilde.com/newsletter
Twitter: @katiwilde
Instagram: instagram.com/authorkatiwilde
Facebook: facebook.com/authorkatiwilde